Someone to Count On

ALSO BY PATRICIA HERMES:

Mama, Let's Dance

You Shouldn't Have to Say Good-bye

Someone to Count On

A Novel by

Patricia Hermes

AN
APPLE
PAPERBACK

SCHOLASTIC INC.
New York Toronto London Auckland Sydney

FIC
HER

ISBN 0-590-22275-9

12 11 10 9 8 7 6 5 4 3 2 1   5 6 7 8 9/9 0/0

Printed in the U.S.A.   40

First Scholastic printing, February 1995

For Kathy, Donnette, Angel,
and Jessica —
who have enriched our lives

Someone to Count On

Chapter 1

Home. I was almost home. The awful school day was finally over, and I was away from that rotten school and rotten teacher.

I turned the corner onto my street and stopped for a moment in front of my apartment. It was quiet there, an afternoon like any afternoon, except that it was September and the first day of school. I stood there on the sidewalk listening, wondering if I could tell just by the feel of it what was going on inside.

We'd been living there for five months now, a long time for us, and I was beginning to like it. Not school — I hated that. But the apartment was nice, and I had made two friends in the neighborhood: Michael and Jason Ogden, who lived down the block. Funny, but for some reason, I always make better friends with boys than with girls. Sometimes I've wondered if I had a regular home like other kids, if I would have more friends, but I suppose it's dumb to wonder about things you can't really know — know, or do anything about, either.

I shifted my books around in my arms and used my key to let myself in.

Elizabeth, my mom, was sitting at the kitchen table stirring a bowl of some goop. Actually, she wasn't *at* the table, but *on* it. And the goop stunk.

"Elizabeth!" I said. "What now?"

She held out a spoon to me. There was green stuff on it, slimy-looking green stuff. "Try it!" she said.

I shivered. "No thanks. What is it?"

"Alfafa," she said. "Alfafa stew." She said it with the same brightness in her voice that normal people use to say, "Brownies" or "Hot fudge sundae."

"Great," I said. "Alfalfa stew. The perfect end to the perfect day."

She raised her eyebrows at me. "Want to tell me about it?" she said. She pushed aside her box of paints and an oily rag — from her latest hobby, even though she calls it her "passion!" — and patted the table beside her. "Here. Sit," she said.

I didn't want to sit. I'd been sitting all day in school. I just shook my head, then moved over to the refrigerator and stood leaning against the door. The door thrummed with the pulse of the refrigerator, as if it was a live thing — friendly, quiet, steady. Toby, my little dog, came out from under the table, circled twice, then collapsed on top of my feet. I crouched down and scratched his lumpy head.

"So, Mr. Beard, my new teacher?" I said. "He hates me."

"Already?" Elizabeth said.

I had to laugh, because she was right. I'm always on the bad side of teachers, always. I never mean for it to happen, but it just seems to work out that way.

"Is that really his name?" she asked. "Beard?"

I nodded.

"Does he have one?"

I shook my head.

"Too bad," she said.

"So listen to the dumb way he talks," I said. "He stares at me and goes, 'Samantha!' — he actually calls me that even though I told him it's Sam — he goes, 'Samantha, could you do us the favor of pretending to pay attention?' He's teaching us to use the dictionary, like we didn't learn that in third grade! Then he goes, 'Samantha, will you be so good as to refrain from sighing heavily when you're asked to participate?' Like I can help it, right, like I don't have to *breathe!* Then, 'Samantha, would you like to have your parents summoned to school' — 'summoned,' can you believe it? — 'to discuss your behavior?' And I didn't really do anything bad, just a little accident. I think he means it, too. He's going to call you."

Elizabeth shrugged. "Big deal." She lowered her eyelashes and smiled, the way she usually only looks at men. "Is he cute?" she asked.

"Cute? He's *old*. He did sound like he meant it, though. He's going to call."

And then, as if we had planned the timing or something, the phone rang.

Both Elizabeth and I stared at each other, then at the phone.

It rang again, and Elizabeth slid off the table and went to answer it.

She said, "Yes," and then "No" and "What's that?" and then "*Rug?*" and "Really?" and then "Spell it."

I had no idea what it was all about, but I could tell it wasn't Mr. Beard.

Elizabeth was half smiling as she talked, twirling the phone cord and bopping around a little, waving her arms and pretending she was directing an orchestra. She hadn't done that for a while, but about a year ago she wanted to be an orchestra leader. She even tried getting into music school to train to be one, but it didn't work out because she doesn't know how to read music.

Watching her, I thought how cute she looked and acted, like a little kid, really. She was wearing shorts and a T-shirt, and her hair was pulled up on top of her head in a kind of ponytail. Her body is curvy, but little, and she's cute. Really cute. When I was little, it was fun having a mother who was different, sort of like having a big sister, one I could have fun with but who didn't boss me around. Even the way she had me call her by her first name was fun. I don't ever remember calling her Mom. But sometimes, I'd been finding myself wishing she was more like other people's moms.

Then I'd feel guilty for thinking that. She didn't grow up with a mom herself, and she says that's why she never learned how to be one. But she says that's good, because most moms are boring. And her dad, my grandfather, I guess he was all right when she was little, but they never liked each other much after that. He has a great big ranch out west, and even though he sends her money, they hadn't spoken to each other since before I was born. I'd never been out west, and I didn't know one single thing about him except that he and I have the same name: Sam. Only he's plain Sam and I'm Samantha. Just once, a very long time ago, Elizabeth had gotten real talkative and described the ranch to me: mountains, trees, cattle, horses, elk — even mountain lions — and I'd immediately fallen in love with it. That was when I began secretly dreaming about my grandfather. I dreamed he sent for me to come live with him on his ranch. That was my home, I pretended — the place where I would stay and never have to move again. I'd never be left alone again overnight, and I'd have friends I could invite home, and we'd ride horses and have tea parties and play with dolls — although of course, I didn't dream that part about the tea parties and dolls anymore!

Anyway, things have been tough for Elizabeth, so I try to be patient with her.

In a minute, she put down the phone. "Rug cleaning," she said. "He wants to come clean our rugs. 'Rug?' I said. 'What's that? How do you spell it?' And you know what? He actually *spelled* it for me."

"That's mean!" I said.

"Well, I didn't do it to be mean, darling! I just couldn't help it." She bent her fingers into claws and widened her eyes like a TV Dracula or something. "I had . . . an irresistible . . . urge!" she said, laughing. Then she added, "Imagine having to sell stuff on the phone for a living."

"I can think of worse things," I said. "Like being a teacher."

"And having you in my class."

I looked at her, but I couldn't tell if she was joking or not.

"That, too," I said.

Elizabeth started to get on the table again, but before she could, the phone rang.

"Rug cleaner again," she said. "Selling dictionaries this time." She went and picked up the phone, and her eyes opened wide and she made pointing signs to the phone. "It's him!" she mouthed at me.

"Mr. Beard?" I whispered.

She nodded.

She listened, and then said, "No, no she's not, Mr. Beast."

I slapped a hand over my mouth to keep from laughing out loud.

"Oh," Elizabeth said. "So sorry. Mr. *Beard*. Of course. Well, Mr. Beard, I'm sorry but Sam's mother isn't at home at the moment."

She frowned slightly, and I knew just what she was going to add — she was going to tell him about my father.

I'm used to questions about my father, especially from kids at school, asking about a dad I don't have. Still, I hate having to say the words.

I started humming so I wouldn't hear her say it either. But I couldn't help it. I don't know whether Mr. Beard asked or not, but she sure told him, in a clear voice that I couldn't help hearing.

"And," she said breezily, "Sam's father isn't available either."

Isn't available. Her way of saying *dead*. But I guess it's as good a way as any to describe a father who fell off a speedboat and drowned himself a month before I was born.

"No," she said. "I'm the housekeeper."

She held her crossed fingers up in front of her for me to see, as if she still believed telling a lie with your fingers crossed is okay. "Yes," she said. "I'm sure she'll get the message."

Then she hung up, her face practically purple from trying not to laugh.

She went directly to the little mirror that hangs above the sink.

She stared into it. "Mrs. Leonard," she said,

laughing at her reflection. "Mr. Beast — I mean Mr. Beard — wants you to know that he's *summoning* you to a conference about your daughter as soon as possible. She needs some discipline and some lessons in good behavior."

She turned to me. "There!" she said. "I gave me the message." She came back to the table. "Boy," she said, "does he sound mean."

"*Sound* mean? He *is* mean! How am I going to stand it? It's just the first day of school. I'll have him all year."

"Unless we run away," she said.

I just looked at her, my heart gone absolutely still. "What?" I said.

"Run away from home," she said. "Have an adventure!"

I took a deep breath.

Leave. Again.

"Really?" I said slowly. "Where this time?"

She shrugged. "We'd find places."

Anyone who didn't know her would think she was joking. But she wasn't — I could tell. We'd taken other trips like this — all of a sudden, all of them fun on the way out. All of them silent and withdrawn and distracted coming home. Like the time when she called herself Lizbet and was going to be a dancer and we went all the way to New York, only to find out there was no apartment we could afford and no one wanted a dancer who was as small as she is anyway. Or the time she was Beth and was going to be a sculptor and we lived in this smelly room surrounded by plaster models. The models kept falling apart while we were sleeping and "Beth" would wake up in the morning and weep over them as if they were dead or something. Or the time she called herself Bethany and was going to study Zen and be a great teacher and we lived in this freezing-cold room in the Maine Woods for a whole winter and I got pneumonia and ended up in the hospital.

It was after that time that I began to wish she just wanted to be called Mom.

I took another deep breath — slow, easy, trying to calm myself. No sense arguing with her. If she made up her mind, we were going, unless I wanted to put up with her sulking for the next six months.

Well, school stunk.

"What's your plan?" I said. "Where will I go to school? Or won't I go? And what should we do about the apartment and stuff?"

"What about the apartment?" she said. "We'll just leave it. It's all rented stuff anyway, practically. And no, you wouldn't have to go to school. I'll teach you myself for a semester. Why not? I'm smart enough."

She is. About book things.

"So how come now?" I said. "What's happened?"

She went to the window and began pinching leaves off one of her herb plants on the sill. "Oh, nothing in particular. Just thought we'd go mooch around."

She couldn't fool me.

Gently, I slid my feet out from under Toby. I pushed

myself off the refrigerator and picked up my books from the counter. "Come on, tell me the truth. How come now? Is it your painting?"

"Oh, Sam!" she said breathlessly, whirling to face me. "Sam, I didn't want to tell you till I was sure. But the letter came today. I'm finally about to give you something you've always wanted."

Something I've always wanted?

She spun across the room to me, whirling dancing, her arms outstretched like a ballet dancer's — like Lizbet's. But when she got to me, just as I thought she was about to throw her arms around me, she paused a step or two away.

She does that a lot — looks like she's just about to hug me, but doesn't. Or maybe I just imagine it. I don't think she's ever hugged me in my whole, entire life, although I know she loves me.

She stood in front of me now, staring at her bare feet, tracing a circle with one foot on the tiles. "Sam!" she said softly. "I know what it's like to be you, I really do, living with a mother who's always on the move. I do know. When all you want is . . . is . . ." She looked up at me. "What do you call it?"

A home.

But I didn't say the word. Because she was up to something, I knew, and it wasn't going to be a home for me.

"Security!" she said triumphantly. "You didn't know I knew, did you? You want to settle down, right?"

12

I didn't answer.

"Well, I got the letter, just today," she went on.

She danced back to the table and picked up a piece of paper and waved it at me. "Here!" she said. "It came today. From your grandfather. From Colorado, the ranch. Along with a big check. It says, 'Come'!"

To Colorado? To my grandfather? We were going to my grandfather's? "How come?" I said.

"Because it's time to make up. I wrote and he answered. It says so right here: 'Come.' " She made a face at the letter. "Actually, it says, 'Come if you must,' but that's just because he's so gruff. And if it turns out good, we'll stay. Permanent. All right?"

I shrugged.

"Now, I'm going to be totally honest with you," she went on, turning away and picking at one of her plants again. "It is near that painting school I've been telling you about, that southwest art school."

Ah-hah!

"But that's not the reason!" she said, turning back to me. "Really. It's for you."

I looked at her.

"So," she said, "living on the ranch sound good? What do you think?"

What did I think?

I thought . . . I thought . . . Did I dare think what I was thinking?

"We're going to the ranch first?" I asked. "Then after that, you'll check out the school?"

She nodded. "Right. You want to go?"

I took a deep breath. "Yes," I said. "Yes, yes, I do."

And as soon as I said it, my heart started pounding like crazy because it was true. I did want to go. A hope, a plan, was forming. And if it worked out, this time, this trip, would turn out to be very, very different.

Chapter 2

I lay awake that night staring at the ceiling and thinking about my plan, thinking about the trip, thinking about my grandfather. I'd never met him, never talked to him on the phone, never seen a letter or even a photo. I knew he sent a check every month, but there was never a letter or anything with it. All I knew about him was that he and Elizabeth had had a big fight once, before I was born. When I used to ask about it, about why they didn't talk, Elizabeth only said, "I have my reasons."

"What reasons?" I asked once.

I remember how she just rolled her eyes and told me not to ask dumb questions.

I didn't think the question was dumb, though; I don't think any questions are dumb, and I especially didn't think questions about him were dumb. And now, even more than before, I wanted to know all about him, every single thing she could tell me about him. And I wondered if now that we were going there, if now at last she would.

Thinking about my plan made me scared, though, so I decided that for that night at least, I wouldn't think about it so I could sleep. And then I realized I couldn't help it. I was filled up with thinking. I was so filled up with thinking, I couldn't even read myself to sleep. And I can practically always read — especially since I had just gotten a new L. M. Montgomery book from the school library. I was totally awake now, though, so I just sat up and gave myself over to thinking. But I told myself I would think only about the trip part, not about the rest.

The trip could be fun — the going-away part at least. And I sure wouldn't miss school. I already hated Mr. Beard, and except for Michael and Jason, I didn't have any friends. Even though we always come back to the same town after a trip, still we move from house to house, apartment to apartment, depending on how much money we have and whether or not we get evicted. We've gotten evicted — kicked out — a few times. So even though I'm in the same town, sometimes I'm in Stratford School on the north side, sometimes Melville School on the south. And never for more than a few months at a time. Every time I show up in a school again, the kids laugh, and even the teachers sometimes make mean comments. That day on the playground, I'd heard Lisa — the self-elected class popularity princess — saying her mother had said I was like "a bad penny that always turns up."

I might be that, but I'm also smart. Smart enough to trip Lisa as she came in from recess and to pretend it was an accident. I'd trip her mother, too, if I met her. Mr. Beard had seen it, though, and I think that's the real reason he called, although Elizabeth didn't say he mentioned that specifically. Thinking about Elizabeth on the phone made me smile. She can be really funny sometimes.

I slid down on the pillow, folded my arms behind my head, and stared at the crack that ran across the ceiling. It went clear across the room, starting in one corner and ending in a shadow right above my bed. The shadow was shaped exactly like the head of an Indian — long face, sharp cheekbones, with a kind of halo around his head, sort of a cross between an Indian chief and a saint. Although in the daylight it just looked like a water stain.

Maybe that was what my grandfather looked like — not a water stain, an Indian chief. I'd always imagined that people who live on ranches have a tough look like that.

I stared at the stain, drifting, half dreaming, when suddenly I was wide awake. Toby! We wouldn't go without Toby, would we?

I sat straight up in bed. "Elizabeth!" I yelled.

I could hear her moving around the kitchen, humming, already packing.

"Elizabeth!" I yelled again.

When she didn't answer, I jumped out of bed and ran down the hall to the kitchen.

"Elizabeth!" I said.

She was at the refrigerator, throwing stuff out, tossing it all into a paper garbage bag. No plastic for Elizabeth. Ecology was one of her latest fads — that and health foods.

She looked kind of disheveled, but happy. "I knew you wouldn't be able to sleep," she said. "Me either. Too excited, right? I keep thinking about this trip. We're going to find out all about that art school. I'm taking all my paintings to show, and if I get accepted, I'll be that much —"

"Toby," I said.

"Toby? What about him?"

I looked around the kitchen. Toby was curled under the table, his head resting on his paws, his toy that he always sleeps with right beside him. As I watched, his head slid to the side, falling from his paws with a thud. He jerked a little, then, still asleep, reset his head and began snoring gently again.

I crept under the table with him and scooted him into my lap. He woke up and nudged against me, then fell into that soft, heavy breathing again.

"Toby," I said. "We're not leaving Toby in a kennel, right?"

"Well, not *leaving* him — no, just putting him in a kennel, and then we'll send for him when we're settled."

"No!" I said. "He's not going in a kennel."

"Sam! All that way in the car? He'll get carsick. You know he always does. You remember what happened that time when he threw up all the way to" — she frowned and looked up at the ceiling — "where were we going that time?" she asked.

"He's coming, or I'm not," I said.

"He was fine in the kennel last time!" Elizabeth insisted. "Just fine. Now don't be stubborn. I know how you get ideas into that little head of yours and —"

"Ha!" I said. "He wasn't fine at all! He was awful, and you know it. Maybe he didn't get sick, but it took forever after we got back before he trusted me, before he let me pat him even. He jumped every time I reached out to him. I bet anything they hit him."

"I'm thinking we could find some nice antique shops along the road," Elizabeth said. "I was thinking about it just today."

"No kennel," I said.

"I've always liked antique shops," she went on, "especially the ones out in the country. You know those country farmers, they don't know the value of half the things they throw away. Remember that quil —"

"No kennel," I said.

Elizabeth blew out her breath and turned back to the refrigerator. She slapped a big slab of some sort of cheese into the bag. "A different kennel, then," she said.

"N. O. Kennel," I said. "None. It's both of us or neither of us."

Toby scrambled off my lap and went to sniff the bag.

"All right!" Elizabeth said then, her back to me still. "You win!" She turned to me, sighing, wiping her hand across her forehead, and leaving a smudge of something brown. She blew her hair out of her eyes. "Sometimes," she said, "you act like *you're* the mother."

Exactly. But I didn't say it out loud.

"I'll take care of Toby," I said quietly. "He won't bother you."

She screwed up her face. "Except for the smell."

"Toby doesn't smell!" I said.

I went back down the hall to the bathroom and locked myself in. I opened the medicine cabinet. Elizabeth didn't believe in taking pills and medicines unless they were "natural," she said — whatever that meant. But she had about a zillion bottles of vitamins and stuff in the bathroom cabinet. I was sure there'd be something there for motion sickness. If I gave it to Toby, maybe he wouldn't get carsick. Dogs couldn't be all that different from people.

I found alfalfa tablets and wheat germ and biotin and flavonoids and — and nothing at all that said it was good for car sickness.

Well, I'd go to the drugstore the next day after school. I'd seen stuff advertised on TV.

I unlocked the bathroom door and went back down the hall to the kitchen.

Elizabeth was now on her hands and knees, pulling stuff out of the vegetable bin under the sink.

20

I hadn't seen her do this much housework in a year.

"When we are leaving?" I said to her back.

"How about tomorrow?" she said. "I figure I can be ready by mid-morning." She sat back on her heels. "How about you?"

"In the morning? No way!"

There were tons of things I needed to do — pack my clothes; get my books; pack my private, important things; get the pills for Toby. But most important, I had to visit that place I always stop by before we leave on a trip.

"How about the day after tomorrow?" I said. "Do I have to go to school tomorrow?"

"Probably. I'd forgotten that — you'll need to get your schoolbooks."

"Schoolbooks?"

"Sure, so you can take them with you."

"They don't belong to me. They're the school's. That would be stealing."

"Stealing, schmealing," she said. She raised her shoulders in a shrug, then stuck her head back under the sink. "I pay taxes," she said. She lifted something under the sink and tossed it out behind her — a bag of potatoes that landed with a soggy thud. "Besides," she said, "if you don't study, everyone will be ahead of you when you come back."

A bag of onions followed the potatoes. "I mean *if* we come back," she added.

And what if she came back alone? What about my

plan — if I stayed with her father? Could I really bring myself to do that? Would he be okay to live with?

"Elizabeth?" I said.

"What?"

"Are you looking forward to seeing him — your father?"

"Not really," she said.

"How come?" I said.

"I'm a realist," she said. "It might not work out."

No big deal. I already knew that. Most things don't work out.

I started back to my room. I decided not to worry about the books too much. If my plan worked, Elizabeth could return my books for me. Or if she didn't come back either, I could mail the books back myself.

At the doorway, I turned and looked back at her, still crouching there under the sink. She wasn't throwing things out, though, was just sitting on her heels, her head under the sink, absolutely still.

"Good night," I said.

" 'Night," she answered, but she still didn't move or turn.

It seemed to me she was waiting, waiting for me to say something. But what? Was she upset about something? Maybe I shouldn't have asked if she was looking forward to seeing him. That letter — "Come if you must" — it wasn't exactly a welcome.

Suddenly I thought of something: I had sometimes felt sad that I didn't have a father. But now I thought I knew what might feel worse.

"Elizabeth?" I said.

"What?"

"Don't worry," I said. "He wants to see you."

She backed out, turned, and looked at me.

"You think so?" she said.

"Yes," I said. "Yes, I do. I really think so."

And I hoped — for both of us — that it was true.

Chapter 3

It took Elizabeth and me just one more day of packing and loading the car and cleaning stuff out to get ready. At school, I didn't say a word to anyone about what we were planning, not even to Michael, but I collected as many books as I could without making people notice, and then took the books home and put them in my backpack.

The most important thing to pack at home, besides my books, was my secret box. It was a shoe box, with macaroni shells glued to the sides and top and spray-painted silver. In third grade, we'd made it to give to our mothers for Mother's Day. But I'd ended up keeping mine for myself, because Elizabeth didn't want it. She hated Mother's Day — Hallmark Day, she called it.

The night before we left, before I packed the box, I opened it, looking again at the stuff I've been collecting for years. There's a blue bird's feather, long and pointed and sharp at the end; one red mitten, with a marble inside; my journal that I've been writing in, on and off, for years; a picture of Elizabeth in her wedding dress. She's turned sideways in the picture, a profile, looking like a princess in her high-neck lace gown.

And another picture: me, about two years old. I'm standing in a snowy yard, wearing a one-piece snowsuit that covers me from my head to my toes. A man is crouching in front of me, his hands on my shoulders, sort of turned sideways to the camera. I'm smiling at him, and although you can't see his full face, you can see he's smiling back at me. Even though I know he's not my father, still I keep the picture, imagining that if my father had lived, he'd smile at me, hold me, just like the man in the picture.

There's a report card from first grade, where Miss Morrison, my teacher, wrote "Comments" in the blank part on the back. She probably didn't think I could read what she wrote, since I was too young, just seven. But I could. I had read it then, and I reread it now. It said: "Samantha is extremely bright and well motivated — but motivated only for the things that interest her. Her reading and spatial concepts are far advanced for her age. However, she seems neither well adjusted nor happy with her peers nor her teachers. I strongly suggest some evaluation and perhaps intervention."

Even when I was seven, I knew what that meant. I did have to look up a few words later, but I remember

25

reading it walking home and knowing exactly what she meant: I was smart. And I was a brat.

At the bottom of the box there was a small silver ring with a tiny blue stone in the center. It had been mine when I was a baby, but now I could only get it on my pinky finger.

There was a flat, smooth stone, shaped like a half-moon. And then, at the very bottom, my birth certificate.

I'd taken it from Elizabeth's dresser drawer one day. I don't know why, except I need to have it. It's a kind of pinkish paper, both printed and handwritten, with a raised seal in one corner. It says where I was born, the borough and city. It gives my birthday, the day and month and year.

And my name: Samantha Marie Leonard.

Samantha — Sam — for my grandfather, Elizabeth's father. Marie for my grandmother, Elizabeth's mother.

And Leonard. My father.

That's who I am: Samantha Marie Leonard.

I put everything back inside the box except the ring, and that I put on my pinky finger. It looked pretty there, and it's my good-luck charm for when we go on a trip. Then I put the box carefully at the bottom of my overnight bag, the one for my daily clothes and books and stuff. I wanted to have it by my side, to be sure Elizabeth didn't poke around in it. I'd be embarrassed if she saw the things I was keeping, especially the journal.

And then suddenly I had a thought, and I got the box out again. I took out the mitten, shook the marble out and put it in my pocket, then put the mitten back in the box.

After I had repacked the box and my things, there was just one more thing to do. But I had to wait until after Elizabeth was asleep to do it.

When the house was finally quiet, I got out of bed. It was cold, the first real cold of fall. I grabbed my sweatshirt and jeans, which I'd dropped on the floor beside the bed, and pulled them on, feeling in the pocket to be sure the marble was still there, then put on my sneakers. The moon was full, flooding my room so that the windowsills and floors turned white, and even the corners were dimly lit.

I can never sleep on nights when there's a full moon. A couple of years ago, when I realized that full moons were the only times I lay awake half the night, I was worried. Maybe I'm crazy, I thought, maybe I have moon madness, like I read about once in one of my books — even though I'm not really sure what moon madness is. But crazy, I do think about sometimes. Once, when I was in third grade, a teacher had screamed at me, "You crazy thing!" And then she'd run out of the room and come back with the principal, just because I'd hit her back when she'd slapped my hand. "Just because you're big," I told her, "doesn't give you the right to hit small people."

I still don't think hitting a teacher was crazy.

I opened my door softly. Down the hall, I could see

that Elizabeth's door was closed, with no light showing from underneath.

I tiptoed across the living room to the front door.

We live in something called a garden apartment, which just means all the apartments are on the ground floor. Outside, our car was backed up on the grass, the front facing the street, the trunk close to the front door for easy loading.

And the trunk stood open — filled with boxes and cartons and my favorite books — wide open. Just inviting burglars!

Really, Elizabeth!

I went outside to the car and slammed the trunk, trying to make the latch click and catch, and trying to do it quietly at the same time.

It took three tries, but finally it was done and I was ready to go where I always go the night before a trip.

Streetlights were on, shining through the trees, making quivering circles of light and shadow on the ground. Between the lamps were pools of darkness.

I passed the Ogdens' house on the corner, bikes and tricycles and Big Wheels strewn across the grass and porch. I pictured the five Ogden kids asleep behind those dark windows — Michael and Jason and all the little brothers — and wondered about their mom. Did Mrs. Ogden love all those kids? She seemed to — always laughing, even wih one kid hanging to her leg, another baby tucked squealing beneath one arm. She seemed happy as she shushed and kissed them and even smacked their bottoms sometimes. And what about Mr. Ogden? Did he love being a dad? He went off to the city every day, but on weekends, he mowed lawns with one of them riding on the tractor with him, or played catch with Michael and Jason. Sometimes I played with them, too. And some days, I saw him bicycling, one little boy in a basket in front of him, one in a basket behind, all three of them wearing helmets so they wouldn't get hurt.

Would my father have done that, too? Elizabeth wouldn't. Not that she wouldn't care. She'd just never think of it. Just like she doesn't think to come home some nights, doesn't think that I'll be worried.

I turned the corner, then crossed the street and turned onto High Street. I passed McCrory's, the dime store, where you can't get anything for a dime, then went past the video store and on to the drugstore. Once, when I was about five years old, I stole a Tootsie Roll from the drugstore. When Elizabeth found out, she laughed and called me a little rascal . . . when I knew she should have been mad at me. And I've never stolen anything since that day, not anything but my birth certificate. If she wouldn't teach me, I'd teach myself.

I stood looking in the window of the store. I had always loved this store when I was a little kid: the smells of medicines, the mysterious stuff in the jars and packages. I even liked being near the old people sitting on chairs in back waiting for their prescriptions, although sometimes they made me feel sad, seeing how shaky and frail they were. And lonely — you could tell that, too — they were very lonely.

I bet my grandfather wouldn't be old like them, though — not shaky-old. I bet he was big and kind of tough looking, like ranchers I'd seen in movies. Or maybe he even looked like that Marlboro ad guy, but older. Maybe he was lonely, too, and couldn't wait for us to get there.

Stupid. That's what I was, stupid. And that's when I made an important decision, standing there looking in that window. I decided it was all right to make this plan. Maybe it was even all right to hope a little. But it was not all right to count on it. I would not count on it. I would not count on him.

Funny. There are not many ways that Elizabeth and I are alike, but we both know that most things don't work out the way you plan.

I turned off High Street and onto the side street, Maple Way. It's a tiny, narrow street, just wide enough for one car. There are no sidewalks though, because there are no houses there, no one who really walks there.

There's a streetlight where High Street and Maple meet, and then not another light for as far down the road as I could see.

I wished I had brought a flashlight, but it was too late now to turn back for one.

I was torn between walking down the middle of the

road, where I could easily be seen if a police car was out, or walking in a more hidden path, but one where anything could be hiding like snakes or raccoons or . . . what? Boogeymen?

I tried to laugh at myself, but I felt a little nervous. I'm always nervous when I come here in the dark.

Since I couldn't make up my mind where to walk, I walked both places, a little while in the middle of the road, then back along the shoulder, where my sneakers and the bottoms of my jeans got soaking wet. Finally, though, I was there — at the gates of the cemetery.

The gates were locked, the way they always are after dark, and I climbed over, just the way I always do. Once inside, I walked down the center path, and when I was far enough away from the gate and the road, I paused and looked around. The moon lit things so brightly it was almost as clear as day. I knew my way by now, but if it hadn't been for playing hide-and-seek with a friend once, I'd never have known about this place, and what was here. And when I did find it, the name practically hidden by the thick vines that grew there, and told Elizabeth, she'd just looked at me.

"Why do you want to bring that up?" she'd said. "That's ancient history."

And that's all she'd ever said about my father's grave — and practically the only thing she'd said about my father, period. Yet I'd noticed that we always came back to the same town when we could live anywhere, and I wondered sometimes if it was because of his grave.

I made my way down the walk, then branched off where the path divides, until I came at last to the stone angel, the angel that sits atop his grave.

The angel is almost life-size, as big as me. I can't tell exactly if it's a boy angel or a girl, because they all wear those dresses, but I think it's a boy. He just sits there, his elbows on his knees, his chin on his hands, not sad, just thoughtful, as though he's waiting. I pretend it's my father, his spirit or soul or something. I think sometimes he knows I'm there, and I even feel that he'd like to talk to me, but made of stone like that, he can't. I bet if he wasn't stone, though, he'd have lots of things to say to me.

Looking at him, I wondered if he already knew I had come to say good-bye.

"We're taking another trip," I said softly. "To my grandfather's, Elizabeth's father. I'm thinking of staying. If he wants me."

I waited, giving him time to answer me silently.

It was quiet there, starlit and peaceful. A few dead leaves had blown around his skirt, and I picked them off and brushed the stone clean with the sleeve of my sweatshirt. Then I said, "Do you think that's a good idea? You won't mind, will you, if it works out, if I like it there, if I like him? It probably won't work out anyway. But if it does, is it all right? You know I won't forget you."

He was still quiet, but then I thought he said it was all right.

For a second, I lay my hand against his face, the angel's face. But very quickly, I pulled away again. It seemed disrespectful or rude or something, to put a hand on his face like that.

I took the marble out of my pocket. I bent over and buried it deep in the vines growing there. "Good-bye," I said. "I'll be back. Even if things work out, I'll be back to visit you, but it may be a while."

I stood up then. "Okay?" I said.

I waited for a long time. And then he said, "Have a good life."

I think that's what he said.

So I left.

Tomorrow — no, today — before the sun came up, we would be on our way.

Chapter 4

It seemed that I had barely fallen asleep when Elizabeth woke me up.

"Morning time!" she said. "Time to hit the road."

I nodded and struggled out of bed.

I started to put on my jeans that were on the floor beside the bed, but they were disgusting, wet and soggy from my trip to the cemetery. I pulled another pair out of my bag, and put them on, then got a plastic bag from the kitchen and wrapped the wet ones and threw them in the back of the car. Then I went to find Toby and give him his motion sickness pills that I'd bought at the drugstore the day before.

First, though, I hid the pills in some dog biscuits. I didn't know the proper dose for a dog, but I figured twice the dose for people should work. I don't know why I decided that, unless because Toby has four feet. Anyway, it sounded right.

Toby didn't mind the pills at all. He just gobbled his biscuits and raced outside for the car.

I had made a bed for him in a big cardboard box on the backseat, and I put him in it with his blanket and the toy he drags around with him everywhere: a chewed-up stuffed dog.

"Bizarre," Elizabeth had said when Toby first attached himself to my old stuffed dog. "He acts like it's his own kid."

Toby didn't seem to care that Elizabeth disapproved, and he always sleeps right next to his own stuffed dog.

After Toby was settled, I got in the front with Elizabeth and put on my seat belt. We had locked the apartment up, then slid the key back into the house through the mail slot in the door. We always did that when we left a place. That way, when the landlord didn't get his rent next month, he'd come and check the apartment and let himself in with his own key. Elizabeth said that was fair, that our rent was paid up till the first anyway, but I thought it'd be better to let him know we were going. Elizabeth said no, he might try to stop us, since I was supposed to be in school.

So we did it her way, and now we were ready.

Elizabeth got in beside me, adjusted her seat, then took a look at herself in the rearview mirror.

Seeming satisfied that she looked okay, she turned on the ignition. "We're on our way!" she said.

"Not till you put your seat belt on," I said.

She rolled her eyes, but she buckled up and then smiled at me. I couldn't help smiling back. She looked so like a kid starting on an adventure.

She had pulled her hair up in that piled-on-top-of-her-head kind of ponytail, with tendrils of hair spilling out in little soft curls around her face and neck. She had hardly any makeup on, just shiny red stuff on her lips and a smudge of blusher along her cheekbones, accentuating the hollows in her cheeks.

She was wearing old jeans and a huge gray sweatshirt turned inside out, and sneakers. Her only jewelry was earrings: a small half-moon in one ear, and a long string of tiny silver stars dangling from the other.

I sighed, then turned to look in the side window, trying to see my own reflection against the night outside. I saw my face, small, thin, triangular, a pointy chin and wide forehead, all angles and bones, my miserable hair tangled and twisted from sleep — awful, flaming red hair. I was wearing jeans and a sweatshirt just like Elizabeth. But where she looked charming and sweet and sophisticated all at the same time, I looked pale and skinny and plain. Very, very plain.

Well, I told myself, if you hadn't been out half the night, you'd look better.

A voice inside said, *Still wouldn't be beautiful.*

Elizabeth backed the car out of the driveway.

Out on the street, she took a look at me. "You excited?" she said.

I nodded. I was. Excited and scared.

But then as we drove, between the rhythm of the

car and my sleepiness from being out half the night before, in spite of all the excitement, I fell asleep. And when I slept, I dreamed.

I was on a ship, going far across the sea. There were things on the ship that scared me, men without teeth, and a sailor standing at the front of the ship looking out, as though waiting for something to come up in front, out of the dark.

I was trying to walk across the deck, when suddenly the ship swayed and something slid out from under a chair. It was a room, and I went in it. I put a hand against one wall, and realized that the wall was giving way. There behind the wall, sitting in a high chair sort of like a throne, was a man with long white hair. He smiled at me, friendly looking, and at first I thought he was my grandfather, and I started to go to him, but then I got scared because I thought maybe he was God — he looked just like the Bible pictures. I wasn't sure what to do, but just then the ship swayed again, and suddenly I was awake. I was in the car, and we were making a huge, sweeping turn onto a highway.

I rubbed my eyes and looked around. It was light — broad daylight.

"Wow! How long did I sleep?" I asked.

"About two, almost three hours," Elizabeth said. "I let you sleep. I was too excited to sleep much last night, and I figured you probably hadn't slept much either."

Right. But all I said was, "Thanks."

"Want to sing?" Elizabeth said. "Pass the time?"

"Sure," I said. I started with one of my favorites. "The sun'll come out tomorrow," I sang.

Elizabeth joined in. "Bet your bottom dollar that tomorrow . . ."

She has a beautiful voice, deep and throaty.

My voice is pretty, too, although not as nice as hers. But I can hit high notes that she can't reach.

We sang for a while, and that made the time pass faster. But when I looked at my watch, it was only eleven o'clock, and we'd been driving since before it was light, probably about five o'clock. I was getting restless.

I turned to the back and pulled Toby up and out of his box to come up front and play with me. I put him on the seat between Elizabeth and me.

Elizabeth inched closer to her door. "If he throws up," she said, "I'll —"

"He won't throw up!" I said.

He didn't seem like he was going to. In fact, it didn't seem like he was going to do anything but sleep. I hoped I hadn't given him an overdose of Dramamine.

I scooped him off the seat and onto my lap, and he nuzzled his head between my legs. I patted his head, scratching him between the ears. "You're okay, aren't you?" I said to him softly.

He just went back to snoring — wheezing, sort of. I did hope he was all right.

I looked over at Elizabeth. I hadn't asked her our route, whether she planned to stop, how long it would take — nothing. I hadn't asked for any plans, not since two days ago when she'd first mentioned going to the ranch. For some reason, I didn't want to know till we were on our way. Maybe I thought that if I knew too much, it would seem too real, or maybe she'd take it back or something. But now it was time, and there were things I had to know. But I was going to start with the safe stuff — our route, the road to Colorado, that kind of thing. Still, even with the safe stuff, I noticed that my voice came out timid sounding when I said, "Where in Colorado? What's the name of the town? What's our plan?"

"Carter," Elizabeth said. "Carter, Colorado."

"Carter? That's the name of the town? That's his name."

"Right. Ranch. Town. All the same."

"You mean," I said, "the whole town is named after him, after his ranch? Does he own the town?"

She shrugged. "Sort of."

"Is he rich?"

She nodded. "Sure." She reached under the seat then and pulled out the bag of maps we keep under there. On top of the pile was a brand-new Colorado map. She handed the bag to me. "See?" she said. "I got a proper map."

I laughed. "But I bet you don't know how we're getting there," I said.

"I bet I knew you'd figure it out for me," she said.

I would, too. I'm good with maps. I always do the figuring of our routes.

I unfolded several maps, finding the best route: first

down through upper New York State, then west across the state, then on and southwest to Colorado — to the town of Carter. It was there on the map: Carter, Colorado!

I looked out the window for a route sign to see where we were — on a highway, a pretty big one, running through countryside. Route 90, the route I would have chosen. Elizabeth might not know how to get there, but she did know how to start out.

When I had planned out what looked like the best route, I folded the maps inside out so the route showed, then set them aside and looked out the side window.

Rich. My grandfather was rich. So it wouldn't be a big burden to him if I stayed there. And ranches always had horses, and maybe he'd take me horseback riding, would make me wear a helmet so I wouldn't get hurt. And what if, after he had found out we were coming, he had prepared a room for me, painted yellow, suncolor, and it was already filled with books? And what if . . .

What if I stopped being a jerk! Fantasy is no substitute for truth — I learned that from living with Elizabeth. And I had made a pact with myself just the night before not to count on this. You can't count on fantasy.

I took a deep breath and turned away from the side window to face front. "Elizabeth," I said, "tell me about him. What's he like? You never say anything, and now that we're going to meet him, I should know."

"What's to know?" she said. "He's a difficult man."

"Why difficult?"

"Why? How do I know why? Because he is."

"But you want to go there, right?"

"I guess."

"You guess! Well, what are we driving halfway across the country for if you just *guess* you want to see him?"

"I told you," she said. "It's been too long. It's time to see if we can't make up. So we're going to try it. Besides, like I said, it's convenient."

Try it? With someone difficult? I didn't want someone difficult. I wanted someone to like, someone who would like us. Someone who would like me.

I waited a while, but Elizabeth didn't say anything more.

I had never for a minute believed Elizabeth about wanting a permanent home for me. I knew that was an excuse to make me want to go. But then if she hated going to the ranch so much, hated him so much, why were we going there at all?

And then I had a terrible thought, one so awful that it made me suck in my breath as if I had a real pain. I tried to push it away, but it stayed, nagging at the edges of my mind in spite of me: was *she* planning to leave *me?* Was she going to drop me off so she could go to her painting school without me? Did she want to dump me? She'd left me a few times before, but just like overnight, like if she went to a party or something — and that one time when I didn't know where she went, that time that scared me so. But this seemed different.

I'd been having this fantasy of a real home, a permanent home — with or without her. But I wanted to choose it.

I didn't want her to dump me.

I took a quick look at her.

She had twisted the rearview mirror and was applying lip gloss, looking at herself in the mirror, then quick back at the road, then back at herself. She was going to run us right off the road if she didn't pay better attention.

I reached over and held the wheel for her. She finished with the gloss, then she put one thumb and one finger on either side of her mouth in the corners. When she seemed satisfied that her mouth was okay, she gave a quick tug at the mirror, jerking it back into place.

"Thanks, sweetie," she said to me, putting both her hands back on the wheel. "Listen, it's been a long time. Maybe he's changed."

"Maybe he hasn't," I said softly, and I have no idea why that popped out.

"You are *so* negative!" she snapped. "Really! How did I ever get a daughter who's so different from me? I look on the bright side. Always. Expect the best, and it falls into your lap. Expect the worst, you get the worst."

But she had just said herself that he was difficult!

She drew in a big breath, and reached out and rested

a hand on my leg. "I didn't mean to snap at you. It's just that he's hard to describe."

She turned and smiled at me then. Her eyes looked misty and her hand stayed on my leg.

I waited till she looked back at the road, then I moved my leg out from under her hand, making a big thing of needing enough room for Toby. I didn't want her to get mushy now. She does that sometimes, getting all sentimental about how sweet I am and how she's not a good-enough mom.

"You weren't snappy," I said.

"Well, I was," she said.

"Okay, you were," I said. "So don't talk about him. Instead, tell me about the ranch."

She laughed. "You are the cutest thing. Okay. The ranch? Well, let's see, it's just a ranch. Hills, tumbleweeds, dirt, tumbleweeds, more dirt. There are horses and elk and deer and dogs. More dogs than people out there, if it's anything like it used to be. In fact, come to think of it, Sam probably likes dogs better than he does people. He sure loves his ranch better than people."

Would he like Toby?

"Does he like all animals?" I asked. "Did you have pets?"

"One," she said. "I had a parakeet named Petie. I'd hang his cage in the tree outside the kitchen window in the summer because I thought he could pretend he was free, nesting in a tree." She laughed. "I was a weird little kid."

"Did you climb the tree?" I asked.

"Me?" she said. "I hate the outdoors — you know that. All that empty space gets on my nerves. Maybe that's one reason Sam and I never got along. Anyway, after a while, Sam had the tree chopped down."

"How come? If it was the tree that Petie —"

"You never asked Sam why he did anything," Elizabeth said.

"Did Petie have to come in then?" I asked.

"Petie got pneumonia and died," Elizabeth said.

"How'd he get that?" I asked.

"I don't know how. He just did. Birds do."

I looked down at Toby in my lap. He was being awfully sleepy, and his breathing seemed even wheezier than before. "Do dogs?" I asked.

"Sure. Dogs do, people do."

"I *know* people do!" I said, mad-like. She could have lied about the dog part.

"Well, it's true," she said.

"Are we going to drive all day?" I said.

"As far as we can. After that, we'll make a schedule. You can plan it. How many miles from here to Denver? The ranch is maybe two hundred miles outside Denver."

I looked at the legend on the map — ten miles to the inch. Using the top half of my thumb as an inch, I tried to figure it, but it was too hard. It looked like a billion miles to me.

"Can't figure it now," I said. "Wait till we stop. I'll write it all down."

"Okay," Elizabeth said. "We'll stop as soon as we can find a place. And we'll go as far as we can each day, all right?"

"Fine with me," I said.

The sooner we got there, the sooner my plan could begin. But for now I was tired of the car, and tired of Elizabeth. And I was worried and confused, too — about her feelings about him, and about the real reasons why we were doing this, and about whether or not she was right about him being difficult. I figured that if I worked at it, I could probably get him to like me. But if he really was that difficult . . . Anyway, I was worried. I guess having been out half the night didn't improve my mood any.

"Toby's tired," I said. "He's had enough for one day, haven't you, Toby?" I took his little head between my hands. "Right?" I said to him.

As if in answer, there was this rumbling sound from deep inside him, and he let out this awful smell.

"To-*by!*" I said, laughing, and I waved my hands in front of my face.

"Oh, gross!" Elizabeth said.

She rolled down her window, and cold air rushed in.

"Told you he'd had enough of the car for today," I said.

And as if to prove that I was right, Toby leaned away from me and over against Elizabeth, his head sort of lolling in her lap. And then, very neatly, he threw up.

Chapter 5

Toby managed to end that day in the car in a hurry. We checked into the next motel we came to, even though there was a huge sign outside that said No Pets!

I hid Toby under the blanket in his box and smuggled him into the room along with our suitcases and my backpack.

Nobody even noticed.

But boy, was Elizabeth ever mad — at him and at me, too, for bringing him up front with us.

And next morning when we got back in the car, Elizabeth wouldn't even turn the key in the ignition until I put Toby in his box and put his box in the back. Not that I could actually blame her. I'd have wanted him back there, too, if it had been my lap he'd thrown up in.

Anyway, Toby didn't throw up anymore. And for days after that, we drove as far as we could for as long as we could. I could see that Elizabeth got tired driving, but I could also tell that she wanted to get this over with just as much as I did. We drove along Route 90 and then along Route 80 till forever it seemed like, through Illinois and Iowa and then into Nebraska. Always with fields full of cows and leftover cornstalks, and roads filled with trucks. The trucks were bringing cows and sheep in one direction — we could see them through the open sides of the trucks — and then other trucks going in the other direction, bringing slaughtered cows and chicken parts to somewhere else, as though nobody was satisfied with being where they were. Like Elizabeth and me, all of us going someplace else.

For four more days we did that, four days in the car, four nights in motel rooms, each time trying to hide Toby since practically all hotels had the same rule: no pets.

The hotels were all the same in another way, too: ugly. Since I was in charge of the money like always — Elizabeth has no money sense at all — it was my decision and we could have stayed in more expensive places. But why pay for expensive rooms when all we wanted was a bed and a shower? I did pretend to myself sometimes, though, that we were stopping at a really fancy hotel with an indoor pool. In reality, every motel room was pretty much the same: the furniture cracked, the drawer pulls broken off or else the drawers so stuck you couldn't open them, the carpet stained next to the bed or by the bathroom door, as though someone had thrown up there. And every bed sagged on one side, and I swear they all had the same orange bedspread. It was as if the bedspread got in a car each morning and raced to the next place ahead of us. Still, it was a place to sleep.

On the day when we had finally passed Denver, it was still light when we stopped for the night, just a little bit after four o'clock. We had decided to drive right through Denver and out into country again before we stopped. The motel we found was right on the highway, and there were a bunch of huge tractor-trailer trucks parked out back. I've always taken that as a sign that the motel wasn't too bad — and that it was cheap. But even though we were on a highway, it was really out in the country, with nothing around but fields and hills and mountains in the distance.

It would be our last night before reaching the ranch. According to my figuring, we had just about two hundred miles to go next day — over the mountains, through the Eisenhower Tunnel, up and over Rabbit Ears Pass. Down into the valley and on to the ranch. To meet my grandfather.

Just thinking about it made me nervous. I was not counting on anything. But I was nervous.

After we checked in that day, Elizabeth wanted to take a nap, but I needed to get out and walk or run. I was so sick of the car. And I was worried about Toby, too. He should get at least a little bit of exercise each day, and all he was doing was sleeping in his box.

When Elizabeth fell asleep, I got my jacket and

shoes and Toby's leash, tucked Toby in the crook of my arm under my jacket, and went outside. I put a paperback copy of *Charlotte's Web* in the pocket of my jacket, too, just in case I found a spot to sit and read a while — even though I'd read *Charlotte's Web* thirteen times already.

I went around back, out of sight of the office, then let Toby out and set him on the ground. He started jumping straight up in the air and then down, as if he was on springs, yipping with little joyful noises.

"Hush!" I said to him. I put my hand around his soft muzzle, my thumb on top, my fingers under his chin. I held his mouth shut tightly.

"You want to be heard?" I asked him.

I made him shake his little head no — back and forth, back and forth.

"All right, then," I said, letting go of his head and snapping his leash on him. "Then shush up."

It was getting dark, and the sky was low looking, that gray, heavy look that it gets in winter when a storm is coming. The wind was blowing sharply, turning the leaves so their bottom sides were up — "showing their petticoats," was what Mrs. Ogden said about that. A drop of rain hit my nose, and after a minute, another. But that was all.

I didn't want to get stuck way out there in a rainstorm, though, so I promised myself we wouldn't go far. Toby was so happy to be out of the car and free that he scrambled through the weeds and grass, making little puffs of dry leaves fly up behind him. He kept tugging me to go different places, and he stopped every few feet, lifting his leg and peeing everywhere. I started counting how many times he did it. Seventeen after I started counting, and he'd done it a lot before I started. There couldn't be anything left inside for him to pee with.

When I found a hill and a small stand of trees, I thought it'd be safe to let Toby off his leash a while.

I unleashed him, then picked up a stick and flung it as far as I could toward the line of trees.

"Get it, Toby!" I said. "Go on, get it!"

Toby took off, his little legs pumping, scattering dry leaves as he went.

He found the stick, snatched it up, and raced back toward me, the stick between his teeth. But as soon as he got back to me, he circled away again. He'd come real close, then prance sideways away again, staying just out of my reach.

"Silly dog!" I chased him, caught him, and wiggled the stick loose from his mouth.

It was all wet and slimy.

He stood there watching me, barking, asking me to throw it again.

I held the stick high, prepared to throw it.

"Ready?" I said.

He stayed still as a statue, ears pricked, legs planted, eyes fixed on the stick.

I made a big throwing motion, looking toward the far hill.

"Get it!" I said.

But instead of letting the stick fly, I quickly hid it behind my back.

Toby took off up the hill, his legs pumping, his stubby tail straight up. But when he got to the top of the hill, he stopped, and started barking. He dug through the leaves, circling and barking, digging and barking. While I stood with the stick, laughing.

"Toby!" I said. "Look!" I held the stick out to him.

He came racing back to me. But instead of prancing around, he just sat down at my feet and whined. His little tail switched back and forth in the leaves, but I swear he was frowning, that he felt foolish and hurt.

I scooped him up in my arms. "I'm sorry," I said. "I was just teasing. You are kind of dumb, though."

He licked my ear.

"Yuck!" I said. "But I'll make it up to you."

I set him down, snapped his leash back on, and we set out walking again. We walked along the highway inside the guardrail, up on the grass. We went a long way without seeing any cars or anything or anyone. It was really very lonely out here. Yet I felt peaceful and even happy, away from everyone, with Toby and the trees and the autumn kind of sky. Way off in the distance, I could see the mountains with the early snow. They stuck way up into the sky, like nothing I'd ever seen back home. And it was all so open — just hills and mountains and that huge sky. We passed some cows off behind a fence, some of them on a hill, some of them in the valley, but all of them facing the same direction, as if there was a silent message at work inside each of them, something calling them home.

Would my grandfather still have cows and steer and stuff the way he'd had when Elizabeth was little? Or was he too old to work on his ranch? But if he was rich, he probably had other people to take care of them for him.

I looked at my watch. We'd been walking for half an hour. It was time for Toby and me to be heading back.

"Come, Toby," I said. I turned and headed the other way.

Toby seemed reluctant, or tired maybe. He just kept stopping, sitting down, and panting.

I bet he was thirsty. I wished I had thought to give him a drink before we left.

I let him rest a moment as I stood watching the sky.

A hawk was circling — drifting, letting the currents carry him round and round and again around. He never moved his wings, just shifted slowly, almost dreamily, side to side.

"What's he thinking?" I asked Toby. "What do we look like from up there?"

But Toby was like that stone angel — no answers. And thinking of the stone angel made me think again of my father. "I'll be back," I whispered to him, looking up at the hawk, still drifting up there. "I'll be back — I promise."

Toby was still sitting in the grass, and I bent and

scooped him up. "Lazy dog," I whispered to him. But I was just joking. Toby is old — ten in real years, seventy-something in dog years. I guess I'd get tired walking if I was seventy, too.

It had begun to rain a little more steadily by then. I tucked Toby inside my jacket, and zipped the zipper partway up, letting Toby's little face peer out. After just a minute of holding him snuggled against me like that, I heard him snoring.

"Silly dog!" I whispered to him.

It was getting dark quickly, and I began to wish I hadn't come so far. I had to watch my step carefully, watching the ground and watching my footing, so that I was almost on top of the deer when I looked up and saw him standing there, watching me.

I stopped short.

He stood at the very edge of a path through the woods, and I had to stifle back a cry that leapt up in my throat.

Huge! He was huge.

We eyed each other, neither of us moving. He was so close that I could have reached out and touched him.

Would he hurt me? Do deer hurt people? I didn't think so, but he was so big, with enormous antlers branching out on either side of his head. His ears were much bigger than I ever thought from seeing pictures of deer or from seeing them at a distance. But it was his eyes that held me, that even reassured me. They were big and brown, almost liquid looking and very wide and soft. He looked to me to be not at all afraid.

I don't know how long we stayed like that, just watching each other, neither of us moving. But after a while, I found myself moving toward him, not even meaning to, just feeling drawn to him.

I took a step forward and then another.

He didn't back up, didn't turn and run. He just tilted his head slightly to one side, as though asking what it was I was doing.

I didn't know what I was doing. I only knew that I wanted to be closer.

Then I remembered Toby, asleep inside my jacket. I held him closer, praying that he wouldn't wake up, that he wouldn't bark.

I reached out a hand. Still the deer stayed there. But his tail was moving.

I stopped.

I remembered the book *Bambi*, and the movie, too — how when the mother deer was killed, a buck, a father deer, spoke to Bambi. He had a beautiful voice — deep, commanding, loving.

It seemed that this deer almost *could* speak.

"You are so beautiful," I whispered to him.

Whispered. But it was a mistake — because at the sound of my voice, he whirled.

"No! Don't go!" I said.

But he did. His tail flicked white, his beautiful body lifted gracefully, and he cleared the small fence and was gone.

He was gone, and it was my fault. I shouldn't have

spoken. Only a vine, trembling a few feet in front of me, gave any hint that he had even been there.

Stupid, but I felt like crying.

Just then Toby woke up and wriggled against me. I tucked him closer to my side and started back to the motel.

All the way back, though, I kept thinking of that movie, thinking about the deer father, pretending I could hear him speak to me.

Chapter 6

Next morning when Elizabeth and I got in the car, we were both really quiet. In fact, the last two days we had been awfully quiet. It was as if the closer we got to the ranch, the more time we spent thinking. But we kept our thoughts to ourselves.

I didn't know what Elizabeth was thinking, but for me, I was anxious. This was the day, the day we'd be there. I kept telling myself that this was no big deal, that if I liked him, it would be fine, if I didn't like him, that would be fine, too. But I still felt nervous: what if I liked him but he didn't like me? Would I be able to make him like me if I tried?

It made my head ache, just thinking about it. Although maybe it wasn't just the thinking that gave me a headache — maybe I was getting a cold or an allergy, because besides the headache, my nose was stuffed up and runny, all at the same time. I had already used up half a box of tissues.

I could tell Elizabeth was nervous and distracted, too, not only because she was quiet, but because of the way she kept rubbing her left arm with her right hand, up and down, up and down.

As we drove, I decided to concentrate on the scenery, trying to see if the mountains were really red, because that's what the word *Colorado* means — colored red, named for the red earth. But although the road was beautiful — curving around mountains that sloped gently up, and up, and up, away until they met the sky — all I could think about was today. Today — sometime — we'd be there. I was sick of this car, sick of the trip, and I hoped so much we'd get there before dark. But at the same time, I almost wished we had another day in the car, another day to get ready to meet him.

As if putting it off would make it easier!

Each turn brought us something new. Each turn brought us closer to him. Was Elizabeth wondering what he'd be like, all these years without seeing him? Was she wondering what she'd say to him, what he'd say back?

I looked over at her. The car headlights were still on, even though it was now daylight, and I reached over and switched them off.

"You okay, Elizabeth?" I asked.

"Why wouldn't I be?" she said.

"You're not . . . nervous or anything?" I said.

"No. You?"

Nervous? I was more than nervous. But all I said

57

was, "Elizabeth? What did you call him when you were little?"

"Sam."

"You didn't call him Dad? Daddy?"

"I called him Sam."

"Why?"

"Why not? You call me Elizabeth, don't you?"

"Only because you told me to."

She sighed. "Maybe he told me to, too. I don't remember."

"What else do you remember about him?"

"Why don't you just wait till we get there?" she said. "You'll see him soon enough."

"Does he know we're coming? Today, I mean? Should we stop and call?"

She shook her head. "He knows we're coming. What day or hour won't matter."

It would matter to me, if I was expecting somebody I hadn't seen in over ten years. But I didn't argue.

We had come down from the mountain by then, and the route we were following, Route 40, made a sharp left-hand turn into a town. We could see a few shops and a McDonald's up ahead. "You hungry?" Elizabeth said, slowing.

I nodded, and we pulled into the McDonald's parking lot, parked, and went in. I left the back window open a little crack for Toby.

The McDonald's was practically deserted, the breakfast crowd gone, lunchtime people not there yet. The first thing Elizabeth and I did was go in the ladies' room. I just had to go, but Elizabeth practically took a bath, standing there at the sink. She washed her face and her hands and arms, and then slipped out of her shoes and stuck one foot in the sink.

"Elizabeth!" I said.

I went and leaned against the bathroom door, holding it closed. "Elizabeth! Cut it out! What if anybody came in?"

"Who's going to come in? This place is empty," she said.

She washed and dried that foot, then switched to the other. Then she took a whole bunch of things out of her purse — bottles, brushes, tubes of stuff, a curling iron with scorched hairs twisted around it. She leaned close to the mirror, wearing her looking-in-the-mirror face.

When she saw me watching her, she said, "You ought to fix yourself a little, too. You could look a lot better if you'd try."

I came closer to the mirror, peering at myself. I looked okay, or at least the same as usual. Skinny triangular face, thick tangled-up hair, and a red nose from blowing it so much. The only thing remarkable about my face is my eyes — at least that's what everybody says. They mean my eyes are big. Some people say I have nice hair, too, but I don't. I hate having red hair, hate it even more when people call me Red.

What would my grandfather think of me? Would he care about how I looked? How Elizabeth looked? Is that why she was fussing so?

"I look okay," I said. "Don't I?"

"At least wash your face," Elizabeth said. "And do something with your hair. If you'd just brush it once in a while, or even wet it down, it wouldn't fly around like that."

She licked a finger and moved toward me.

I ducked away from her hand.

I went and washed my face, using the other sink, and got the front of my hair soaked so it lay flat.

When Elizabeth was all finished — and she did look awfully pretty, all curls and eye shadow and cheek blusher and shiny lips — we went and got some lunch. I bought Chicken McNuggets so I could give some to Toby. I had told him I'd make it up to him for teasing him yesterday.

We took our food out to the car. When we were buckled up and I had given Toby his treat, we were off, both of us quiet again.

After I had finished my lunch — and it tasted like straw, no flavor at all, probably because of my cold — I dug in my overnight bag and pulled out my journal. I wanted to read, had missed my books so much, but I get carsick from reading. For some reason, I can write without getting sick, though. I hadn't written in my journal since we started, but when I'm feeling anxious, writing seems to make me calm. Maybe if I wrote all the time until we got to the ranch, I wouldn't worry.

I couldn't think what to write, so I began making up lists of things. I started with a list of things I wished for:

I wish Michael and Jason lived in Colorado.

I wish my grandfather will be extra nice, not difficult.

I wish everything works out at the ranch, and . . .

And what? I wasn't even sure what I hoped for there anymore.

I wish I had a new pair of jeans and I wish I had a bathrobe.

I'd never had a bathrobe.

I wish for Toby to be younger so he'd live a long time.

I wondered if God could do that, make an animal get younger.

I laid the book down on my lap and stared out the window.

When I was in second grade, the year Elizabeth was in her religious phase, I went to a Catholic school. My teacher, Sister Stella, told us that God sits in a big armchair up in the sky and has angels with huge wings floating around him like helium balloons. Well, she didn't say helium balloons, but that's the way I pictured it.

That whole year, I used to lie in bed and picture the angels. I remember waking up one night in the dark and thinking that I saw one of them standing right there beside my bed. It scared me so I started to scream, but Elizabeth didn't come. It was one of the nights she was gone. It was probably just as well, though, because when I finally got the courage to get up and turn on a light, it was so embarrassing. My Guardian Angel was my flannel nightgown hanging on the bedpost.

I sat up and picked up the notebook again and started on another list.

Ways That Elizabeth and I Are Different

Elizabeth likes to move around.
I don't like to move.

Elizabeth does not like her father.
I'm going to try and like her father.

Elizabeth is pretty.
I'm not pretty.

Elizabeth knows how to make people like her.
I'm not sure I know how to do that. (And why doesn't Elizabeth know how to make her father like her? Or maybe she's never tried?)

Elizabeth lies when it suits her.
I lie only when I have to.

Elizabeth likes to drive with the windows up.
I like the windows down, with the noise and air and smells rushing in.

I looked over at Elizabeth, looking for things to add to my list, and saw her looking back at me.

"What's that you're writing, sweetie?" she said. "Schoolwork?"

"No."

"A letter?"

I couldn't tell her I was writing about her and me. So I said, "Wishes. I was writing about what I wished."

I thought she would laugh at me, but she didn't. "Wishes," she said, and she sighed. "I guess wishes are all right. But you know what Sam used to tell me? He'd say, 'If wishes were horses, beggars would ride!' And even though that used to make me mad, I think now he was right. You know?"

I turned and looked out the window. Was he right? Maybe, because if wishes worked, Toby would be a puppy and I'd be wearing new jeans now. But wasn't it good to think about what you wished for? Or else how could you ever know if you were close to getting it or not?

I put my head back against the seat, my eyes closed. I really didn't feel too good. My throat had been aching since that morning, and my eyes felt heavy, scratchy, and rough. And I had blown my nose so many times, it was getting really sore.

"Sweetie?" Elizabeth said. "Sit up. I think we're lost."

She had slowed, and as I sat up, she pulled off to the side of the road in front of a Route 24 road sign.

"Everything's changed so much," she said. "Look at the map. Are we going the right way?"

I looked at the route sign, looked at the map. "We're

fine," I said. "It's been ten miles since our turn onto 24. We're going north. Looks to me like about forty more miles."

"You sure?" she said.

"Sure," I answered.

"Darling," she said, and she smiled at me, "what would I do without you?"

"You'll do all right," I said.

For a long while she sat staring out the front of the car. Anyone else might think we were regular tourists, seeing the scenic view from the scenic overlook. But I could tell from the look on her face that she was seeing something else completely. Her father?

"Sweetie?" she said, still staring out front, not turning to me. "I have something to tell you."

I could feel myself get cold inside. What now?

"What?" I said.

"Sam? Your grandfather? He doesn't know about you."

"Doesn't know what about me?"

"He doesn't know about you, period. He doesn't know I have a daughter."

"He doesn't *know?!*" I turned and stared at her. He doesn't know about me? "Why?" I said. "I mean how come? Why didn't you tell him?"

"I told you — I haven't talked to him since before you were born. So after your father . . . died . . . I was afraid that if Sam knew, he'd want to take you. He never thought I could do anything right. He sure wouldn't think I could raise a kid by myself."

Could she?

"So," Elizabeth went on, "he might be . . . surprised." She turned to me then, smiling, but the smile was stiff looking. "He's going to love you, though. He can't help but love you."

I didn't answer. What could I say? What did I even think? Numb, that's what I felt. This didn't make sense. Would he really have taken me away if she'd told him?

Elizabeth started up the car then, and we pulled out onto the highway.

My head was spinning, aching. I had a fever, a cold. My grandfather didn't know about me. He didn't know I was coming. He didn't even know I was alive.

Would he be happy to know he was a grandfather? Or would he hate that?

I didn't know the answers to those things, but I did know this: since he didn't know about me, he couldn't be looking forward to meeting me.

So what? I hadn't been counting on it.

It took almost an hour until we saw the yellow crossroads sign — Carter's Ranch Road — and neither of us had spoken the whole way.

The ranch. His name was right there. My grandfather's ranch.

I sat up straight and looked all around me, up and down the road, at the barbed wire fence surrounding the fields, at the hills, the cattle. His home. My heart was thumping hard, and I could feel sweat trickle down under my shirt.

"Well," Elizabeth said, turning to me. "This is it. You ready?"

Ready?

No. But ready or not, Elizabeth had turned in and we were bumping our way up the long road to my grandfather, my grandfather who didn't even know I was alive.

Chapter 7

It was an unpaved road, hard-packed dirt, showing signs that it was well used. A pickup truck was bouncing toward us, a man in a yellow slicker at the wheel, another person beside him. The driver raised a hand, waving at us, and then was gone.

I quickly looked at Elizabeth. Who was that? Him? Sam?

But no, because Elizabeth just shook her head.

We went at least two more miles before we had to stop, the road blocked by a gate. There was a tall metal archway over the gate, and high on either side of the arch were two black silhouettes of llamas. Llamas? The words CARTER RANCH were etched into the gate in big black block letters. Just on the other side of the gate, behind a low rail fence, there was a house built into the hillside, with smoke like a gray snake coming up from its chimney.

His house. My grandfather Carter's house.

I swallowed. My house?

Elizabeth stopped the car but didn't turn it off.

"This it?" I asked.

"Yes. Get out and open the gate," she said. "Just lift the bar and push it back. When I drive through, close it after me."

I got out.

It took a bit of tugging and yanking, but after a minute, I was able to lift the bar and pull the gate back so she could drive through.

When the car was through, I closed the gate, letting the bar drop into place. Elizabeth drove slowly the few hundred feet up to the house, and I followed on foot. Even though it was only a tiny way, I felt so exposed, as though anybody in the house could see me and wonder about me trudging along behind the car out in the open . . . especially since they didn't even know I existed. I remembered the deer, and wondered if he felt like this when he came out into the open.

Still, I was curious, and as I walked, I looked around at the rolling hills, the cattle dotting the fields, at the horses running fast behind a fence, chasing one another, it looked like. Horses! He did have horses. But I didn't see any llamas.

Would he let me ride his horses? What if he gave me a horse of my very own!

I looked at the big, sprawly house nestled into the side of the hill. Except for the thin gray chimney smoke creeping upward into the gray sky, there was no other sign of life — no people, no cars. Way back beyond the house was a barn, and I could see a bunch of cows, all of them clumped close together facing out, as if lined up for a class picture.

Cows, horses, but not a single person.

Elizabeth parked in front of the house, then waited for me to catch up with her before she opened the car door.

"What about Toby?" I said as she got out.

"Later," she said.

"I'll be right back," I said to him — not that he seemed to care. He was sleeping.

Elizabeth got out, closed the car door, then straightened her shirt and smoothed her jeans. She smiled at me then and reached for my hand, holding it tightly — something I didn't ever remember her doing before, not even when I was tiny, except maybe for crossing a street or something. Her hand was trembling, though, so I let her hold mine and even squeezed hers back. I even had to admit to myself that it felt good to hold hands just then.

Hand in hand, we approached the front door.

And I thought I'd die because of what she did next: without pausing a second, she pushed open that big heavy door. She didn't knock, didn't ring the bell, didn't do any of the things that regular polite people do. She just opened that door and barged right in.

"Elizabeth!" I hissed at her. "You're supposed to knock!"

She just shook her head at me and pulled me in beside her.

We were standing in a wide, long hallway, dark paneled, with a bench on one side, heavy doors on the other, and a big door at back. All of the doors were closed.

"Anyone home?" Elizabeth called. Loudly.

I pulled my hand free of hers. I wanted to just disappear. What kind of way was this to meet somebody you hadn't seen in a zillion years, barging into their house? No wonder she and he had had fights.

"Hello?" Elizabeth called again. "Anyone home?"

Silence, until suddenly the back door swung open and a big, heavyset woman hurried forward.

Good thing she came when she did, too, or we'd have been eaten by the dogs — two huge golden Labs that came charging at us through a different door, growling deep in their huge throats. They only stopped their charge when the woman said, "Now, quit! You quit that!"

They did — quit charging. But they didn't quit growling. They kept circling us, their big paws padding on the wood floor, making soft rumbling sounds in their throats.

Beautiful dogs! But would they like Toby, get along with Toby?

"Something I can do for you, Miss?" the woman said to Elizabeth.

It was polite enough, the words. But the way she said it, along with the look, made you know that what she really meant was, What do you think you're doing standing in my front hall?

I felt like telling Elizabeth, I told you so!

"I'm Elizabeth," Elizabeth said. "My father around here somewhere?"

"Your father?" the woman said. "Elizabeth?"

That's all she said for a long time, just stood there looking first at Elizabeth, then at me, then back at Elizabeth again.

Elizabeth just stared back.

"Well," the woman said, but she still didn't move. She blinked and looked at me. "And this will be . . . ?"

"Sam," Elizabeth said.

"Sam," the woman repeated.

I saw the look she gave me, looking me up and down, from my tennis shoes with the tiger stripes, all the way up to my hair, and then down again. On the way down, her eyes lingered on my chest. It wasn't much of a chest, at least not yet, but it was there. I knew what she was thinking though, so I helped her out.

"Samantha," I said.

"My daughter," Elizabeth said.

"Well. Well, I'm blessed," the woman said.

She nodded, and then, after a minute, she said again, "Well, I'm blessed." And then she smiled. It was a nice smile, a nice face, broad and plain, and suddenly, I liked her a lot. A nice, plain face, a lot like she was, I bet. She had no makeup on, and there was nothing fancy about her — except for her jewelry. She wore huge, dangly silver earrings with a stone of some kind in the center. She had wide hips, hair tied into a bun, and big faded blue eyes with lots of wrinkles around them. And that broad face with the big smile.

It made me feel comfortable with her right away, that smile did. It might be nice to live in a house with someone like her.

She took a deep breath and turned back to Elizabeth. "Your daddy's here," she said. "I have to warn you: he's not real well, though. I think I'd best go tell him first that you've arrived."

"Don't bother," Elizabeth said. "I'll tell him myself. Where is he?

"No, Miss, I'm afraid —"

"I'm not 'Miss!' " Elizabeth said. "I'm Elizabeth. And who in the devil are you?"

"Elizabeth!" I hissed at her.

Didn't she know, couldn't she tell, that this was not the kind of person you should be using that kind of language to?

"Maura," the woman said, and she straightened herself up and seemed to get taller as she said it. "Maura Cassidy O'Hara —"

"Why don't you go back to the kitchen then, Maura?" Elizabeth said. "Tell me where my father is. Or even better, he's probably in the —"

She started for a door that led off to the right of the hall, but suddenly Maura was in front of her. Maura was big and square, but she moved as lightly as a dancer or a quarterback.

72

"You didn't let me finish, Miss," she said quietly, her whole body blocking that doorway. "It's Maura . . . Cassidy . . . O'Hara . . . Carter."

Carter? Like his wife? My grandmother?

"Carter?!" Elizabeth's hand flew to her mouth, and I saw her eyes widen so that you could see the whites all around the dark blue irises.

Anyone could see that she was surprised. But knowing her, I could also tell that she was mad.

Her father had gotten married. And he hadn't told her.

At the same time, I realized how tired and sick I felt, how my legs were now aching as well as my head. Also, my nose was so stuffy I could hardly breathe. I sank down on the bench that ran along the opposite side of the hall, away from where Elizabeth had been heading, but I kept watching them, watching my grandmother. I've never had a grandmother.

One of the dogs growled a little, but his tail wagged hard, as though he didn't mean to growl but knew he was supposed to. I didn't reach to pat him, though, in case he did mean it, but I let my hand dangle over the edge of the bench so he could sniff it if he wanted. The other dog had lain down by Maura. I just sat and watched Elizabeth and Maura, Maura still blocking the way to the door across the hall.

Elizabeth looked small and thin, almost frail looking up against Maura. She looked especially pretty, too, maybe because Maura looked so plain, or maybe because Elizabeth had spent so much time on makeup back there at the McDonald's. But what was coming through to me so clear was this: Maura seemed okay — comfortable and at home here and kind of pleasant. And Elizabeth was feeling mean.

I knew Elizabeth when she got in one of these moods. I also knew why she got this way — her way of covering up when she was scared. But I knew, too, that when she was in one of these moods she wouldn't listen to God himself. She sure wasn't going to be stopped by Maura Carter. For some reason though, I had the feeling that she had met her match in Maura.

If I didn't feel so tired and achy, I would have been dying to see how Elizabeth and Maura — my mother, my grandmother — would work this out. But I was feeling really miserable by then. I leaned my head back against the wall and closed my eyes.

And that's why I missed it, missed seeing the door open behind Maura, missed seeing the expression on Sam Carter's face when he first saw his daughter standing there in his front hall. Missed the first look at my grandfather.

Chapter 8

I don't know how long he had been standing there. I only opened my eyes because the silence seemed to have gone on too long. What I saw was not at all what I'd expected to see. He was tall — very, very tall — and very thin and very old. He had graying hair combed carefully across his head, pink scalp showing through. Although he was carrying a cane, he stood straight and seemed strong enough, not sickly like Maura had said. His eyes were dark, quick and darting, almost fierce looking, under very black eyebrows. I've never seen eyebrows so thick and bushy, meeting right in the middle of his forehead in a deep, frowning kind of line. He was smiling slightly at the same time, and it made his face look odd, kind of mismatched, like a little kid's drawing.

"It's Elizabeth!" he said. He shifted the cane from his right hand to his left and held the right hand out to her.

She took his hand for an instant, then dropped it. "How've you been?" she said.

"Well," he answered. "I've been well. And you?"

She shrugged. "Can't complain."

Boy! If I had just met my father for the first time in a zillion years, I sure wouldn't say such dumb things.

He turned then and smiled at Maura, and everything about him seemed to change. Where before he was just a tall, frowning old man with a cane, now, looking at her, he was different. He even looked younger. And lots nicer, his eyes soft, not snapping and fierce like before. "You've met my daughter?" he said to Maura, his voice soft, seeming to match hers with that small lilt in it.

"I've met her," she said.

He turned to Elizabeth. "And you've met my wife?" he said.

"We met." Icily.

He smiled broadly at Elizabeth all of a sudden. Even in the dark of the hallway I could see that his teeth were stained yellowish.

Weird, but no one had noticed me. *He* hadn't noticed me — his granddaughter. It was as though I was invisible, sitting on the bench there, like being an audience in a darkened theater. And being invisible like that, all my senses seemed extra sharp, getting feelings from the people around me that I wouldn't have gotten if they'd known I was watching. Or maybe it was the fever that was making me feel things especially strongly. Whatever, I knew exactly what each of them was feeling.

Maura was feeling watchful and puzzled. Sam Carter was amused but maybe a little angry, too. Elizabeth was nervous and very angry. And I didn't understand the why of any of it.

And me, what was I feeling? Worried, I guess. And sick.

I leaned my head back against the wall, and the motion or something seemed to make them all notice me at the same time.

Elizabeth came to me and took my hand, pulling me gently but firmly to my feet. "This is Sam," she said. "My daughter, Sam. Antha."

She added the "Antha" part as if it was a middle name, as if she was suddenly embarrassed about "Sam."

"Samantha?" Sam said, looking quickly at me, and then back at Elizabeth.

He kept staring at her, and even though there wasn't much light in that hall, I could see a dark flush spread up his face.

It was Elizabeth's turn to look amused. "My daughter," she said. "This is my daughter."

Sam turned his fierce eyes back to me then.

Suddenly I heard a voice in my head, something stupid whispered over and over again in my brain. "Like me," the voice said. "Like me, please like me."

I took a deep breath and forced myself to look right at him.

His eyes did the same thing that Maura's eyes had done — looked me up and down and came to rest on my chest. But where Maura's eyes were just plain asking a question, I had the sudden feeling that Sam Carter's eyes were laughing at me.

Failed. I had failed my first test with him.

Sam looked away from me and back at Elizabeth.

"Since when?" he said.

"Since about eleven years," Elizabeth said, laughing. She pushed me forward then. "Say hello to your grandfather."

The way she said it was nice enough, but the words made it sound like I was this little kid about four years old.

I made a face at her. But when he put his hand out to me, I took it.

"Hello," I said quietly.

His hand was hard and callousy, with the flesh so thin I could feel the bones right through, like I was holding the hand of a skeleton. His nails were yellow and curved, coming down over his fingertips like bird claws, but he held my hand tight, not at all like what I expected.

"Samantha?" he said. He had to bend to look into my face, he was so tall. "What kind of name is that?"

How could I answer that? What kind of name? A name a lot like his own.

"Samantha?" he repeated.

"Sam, really," I said. "They call me Sam."

"That's a boy's name," he said.

"It's my name."

He let go of my hand. "What'd you do to your hair?" he said.

"What do you mean?"

"Looks like you combed it with an eggbeater," he said.

I put a hand to my hair. It felt regular, not terribly tangled. I stared straight at his head. "At least I *have* hair," I said.

Sam Carter roared with laughter. It was a total surprise, not just to have him laugh, but because it was such a weird sound coming from him, deep and throaty, almost a growl. He was such a thin person, it was hard to figure how he could laugh like that.

I couldn't help staring at him as he laughed.

After a minute, he took a deep breath and then looked at me again, a different kind of look from before, although I couldn't tell what he was thinking. "True enough," he said, still smiling. "True enough. Let's go in the library. Maura, think we could get some coffee or something in there?"

She nodded and went back down the hall in the direction she had come from.

Sam Carter started to lead the way to a room across the hall, but halfway there he stopped and looked at Elizabeth over his shoulder. He pointed his chin at me. "Her father?" he said.

"Art Leonard," she answered. "You know, the one you couldn't stand?"

"Right again, wasn't I?" he said.

79

He knew my father! Had known my father. Why hadn't he liked him?

Sam shook his head and led the way into the far room.

It was a huge room that we went into — huge and warm and beautiful — and I instantly fell in love with it. It was far better than anything I had pictured, much better than that yellow room I imagined him preparing for me. This was a real library, with the walls lined with books — books and books and more books! There were couches and worn leather chairs gathered around the fireplace. There was a fire going in the fireplace, and the room was warm, not only from the fire, but warm with the look of the place. It smelled of logs burning and of books and tobacco and dogs. Even with the dog smell, though, it was a nice smell. It was the kind of room I'd seen in movies, read about in books, but never dreamed I'd actually, really be in. There were tables piled high with papers and books, and some scattered rugs on the hardwood floor. It was just such a comfortable place that I instantly felt that I belonged there.

If I stayed here, I'd never leave this room.

Elizabeth sat down in a chair on one side of the fireplace, and Sam Carter sat in another facing her. I sank into one of the chairs back out of sight of both of them and watched.

Sam settled into his chair, one long leg bent at the knee, the other one stretched stiffly in front of him like it was a robot leg, all metal and clanky. He had set his cane over to one side, and his hands rested on the arms of his chair. I couldn't take my eyes off those hands. They were just exactly like bird claws, as if he was a parrot. Now that I could see them better, I could tell that it wasn't only the fingernails that were bent, but the first joints of each finger, curved like bony yellow seashells. One hand was doing a little dance, up and down on the arm of the chair, up and down, the nails clicking against the wooden arm. Elizabeth kept watching the hand, and I could tell the clicking was driving her crazy. If I had done that, she'd have yelled.

He knew it was annoying her, too, because every time she looked at his hand, he'd pause with it in midair. When she looked away, he'd let it drop to the chair arm with a loud thunk. Then he'd do it all again: *click-click, click-click.*

Neither of them said anything, not him, not Elizabeth, as if each of them was willing the other to speak first.

In a minute, the door swung open, and Maura came in carrying a large tray. There was a round oak table in the middle of the room, and she went there to put the tray down, but the table was littered with papers and books, and she was having trouble managing.

Nobody moved to help her, not him, not Elizabeth. They didn't even look at her.

I got up to help. I pushed some magazines and papers out of the way, making room for the tray.

"Thank you, lamb," she said. "You drink coffee, don't you?"

She spoke so softly that I had to bend close to hear her.

I didn't drink coffee. But I noticed that there were four cups on her tray, and no glasses — nothing for milk or Coke or anything. So I said yes, I did, and figured that was an okay kind of lie to tell her.

Maura arranged the cups on the saucers, then poured the coffee. She handed me a cup. "Take that to your mama," she said softly.

I took it, and she took one to him, to Sam.

Elizabeth took the cup from me without even looking at me.

He took his from Maura, and he said thanks, not like Elizabeth. But he kept staring at her.

I swear, they reminded me of two dogs circling each other, sniffing, not fighting yet, but ready to tear each other's throats out if one moved the wrong way.

Maura and I went back to the table, and she arranged some rolls on a plate. "You pass these, lamb," she said. She put a finger on one of the rolls — a long, twisty one, sprinkled with seeds and salt. "That's his. He does love his salt sticks. And here's the butter, too. Can you carry it all?"

I nodded and took the rolls and the butter. I decided to serve him first. With the mood Elizabeth was in, it would be just like her to take the only salt stick. And then what would I do?

As I crossed the room, I practiced two words in my

mind — the words *my grandfather*. I had been calling him Sam in my mind, but I couldn't call him that out loud. He was too old for that, and I couldn't even think names like Pop-Pop or Grandpa, like some kids I know do. So I snuck a look at him and tried it in my head: *my grandfather*.

Silently, I shook my head. No, I just wouldn't call him anything for a while.

I held the plate and the butter for him while he buttered his salt stick. It took a long while for him to do it, and I had to stand beside him all that time. He smelled funny — not bad exactly, just old — a mixture of attic and talcum powder. When he was finished, he looked up and gave me a little smile — his first, first at me, anyway.

It surprised me, because even though his teeth were kind of yellow, it was a nice smile, warm for just a second, seeming to light up his face, sort of like when he had looked at Maura before.

Then I took the rolls to Elizabeth. She took one, but waved away the butter. Then she began tearing the roll apart, pulling out all the nice soft part, and eating just the outer part, the crust. I took the plate back to Maura.

I didn't want any rolls. I didn't want coffee either. But I didn't want to hurt Maura's feelings, so I took the cup she poured for me, and poured in lots of milk, too much, until it reached right to the top and over-flowed some into the saucer.

Carefully, I carried it to my chair and sat down.

Maura sat in a low chair next to the fire, feeding bits of roll to the dogs. One of the dogs seemed real dumb to me, kept walking into things and bumping its head.

And that, the occasional sound of the dog or the sound of cup against saucer, or the sound of my grandfather's slurping — for a long time, those were the only sounds in the room.

It was so quiet, as if the quiet itself was a sound. I began to hear other sounds then: my grandfather swallowing, a hard *cluck* sound in his throat, as though two bones were knocking together. *Cluck-cluck* it went, *cluck-cluck*. The hissing of the fire, logs shifting and settling with a sigh. The tick of the clock on the wall behind Elizabeth. Breathing — ours, the dogs, the fire.

"So what do you want?" he finally said. He was feeding a roll to one of the dogs, and I didn't know for a minute if he was speaking to the dog or to us, until I saw him look up at Elizabeth.

"I don't *want* anything," Elizabeth answered. "That's not the right question."

"Then what is?"

She didn't answer.

Sam set down his cup on his small table, and stretched his legs out in front of him.

Suddenly I sneezed, and Sam looked at me sharply. He seemed about to speak to me, but instead, he turned back to Elizabeth.

"Listen," he said, "you write to me out of the blue.

Haven't seen or heard from you in over ten years, although you do cash the checks. Maybe more than ten years, twelve?" He dropped his head back against the chair, squinting up at the ceiling, as though there might be a calendar up there. "All those years and then one day you write and say you want to come. But you want nothing? I don't believe it."

"Some people might say it was enough to want to see their father," Elizabeth answered.

"Some people might," he said, but from the way he said it, there was no doubt that "some people" did not include Elizabeth.

He wriggled his legs again, as if he was trying to find a more comfortable position. When he had re-adjusted, he said, "Let's get something straight. One day, one night really, you walked out of here all those years ago — gone. Not a word to anyone. Not a by-your-leave, just gone in the middle of the night. A note: 'I'm marrying Art. He loves me and I love him.' Next thing I know, you write that the idiot has fallen off a speedboat and —"

"I never called him an idiot!" Elizabeth burst out.

Sam acted as if he hadn't even heard her. "Fallen off and drowned himself," he went on. "Wild, like I always knew he was. Motorcycles, speedboats, rock climbing, jumping out of planes! Only worse than I thought. Not only kills himself, but leaves you with a kid, too. No wonder you never told me. And then not another word. I've tried to reach you — you remember when I used to try — but you never answered a letter or a call. And now you're back. Well, you're welcome here. You're mine and you're always welcome, along with . . ." He stopped and looked at me. There was no softness in his look, though, that fierce frown on his face again. "Samantha there. Welcome as you've always been, even though you pretend not to know I care. But don't try to tell me that there's not a reason for the sudden visit home to Daddy."

"As if I ever called you Daddy!" she said.

He just shook his head.

But he had said we were welcome here! He even said he cared. Did that mean he wanted us to stay?

Did Elizabeth want to stay?

There was another of those long silences. I put my head back against the chair, my hand to my face, holding my napkin as a handkerchief because I could feel another sneeze coming.

"Miss," Maura said quietly. "I think you'd best tend to your daughter. I think she's feeling poorly."

"Sam?" Elizabeth said, turning to look at me. "Something wrong?"

Something wrong? What kind of question was that?

Chapter 9

I was ready to get out of there, ready for someone to show me to a bed, my head was aching so much. But before I could move, the hall door burst open and a kid came rushing in. A small kid. A dirty kid. A kid with Toby in his arms!

I jumped up and practically ran across the room. "Give me my dog!" I yelled. I grabbed Toby away, hugging him close to me. "Where'd you get Toby from?"

I glared at the kid. A boy? A girl?

He . . . she . . . was about my age, wearing dirty jeans and filthy, muddy boots and a knitted hat pulled down so low I couldn't see any hair. The face was dirty, too, a streak of mud across one cheek, but kind of pretty. A girl, I thought, almost black eyes, her skin a beautiful rosy brown.

"Where'd you get my dog from?" I said again, glaring.

"You left him in the car, birdbrain!" the kid said back. "Don't you know better than that? Dogs get heatstroke in cars."

"Right!" I said. "When it's freezing out practically."

The kid glared back at me, coming so close to me our faces were just inches apart. The two huge Labs suddenly began circling us, both of them growling.

"You quit that, you two," Maura said, getting to her feet and coming to us.

I looked at Maura, surprised, because for a minute, I'd thought she was talking to me and this kid. But when she got closer to us, she put a hand on each of the dog's heads, pushing them into a sitting position, and it was clear she was talking to them, not to us.

"Is this your dog, lamb?" she said then, reaching to Toby and putting a hand lightly on his head.

I nodded. "It's Toby," I said.

"Toby," Maura said.

"A dog?" Sam said. "Bring him here!"

Should I?

I looked at Elizabeth, but she wasn't looking back. She was resting her head on her chair as if she was plain exhausted. I hoped she wasn't getting sick, too.

Should I take Toby over to him? What if he didn't like him, said they already had enough dogs or something?

I was standing there, undecided, when the kid reached for Toby. "Give him here."

"I'll do it!" I said. "He's my dog!"

I went back across the room, the kid following. Toby

was wide awake now, ears pricked up, tail wagging.

I stood in front of Sam's chair, Toby still cradled in my arms.

"Put him down. Let me see him," Sam said.

Oh, boy. No way I'd put Toby down, not with those two monster dogs still in the room.

"You have to hold him," I said. "I can't put him down."

"What's wrong with him? Can't hold his own with the big boys?" Sam said. But he held out his long arms for Toby.

Carefully, gently, I lay Toby in Sam's arms, but I stayed close. It's not that I thought he would hurt Toby or anything; it's just that I didn't know what to expect. So I stood close by.

Sam put both his bony hands around Toby, tilting Toby's little head up. "Well, hello, dog," Sam said softly, the most gentle sound I'd heard from him yet. He squeezed Toby's jaw then, making him open his mouth, the way I'd seen the vet do once, as if he was checking Toby's teeth. "So you're old, too," Sam said, releasing Toby's jaw. "And you like to chew on wood, don't you? Or you used to when you were a puppy."

That was true! Toby used to chew on anything wooden — table legs, chairs, woodwork, drawers, anything. He even got us evicted because of it once, when he chewed right through the apartment door.

"How do you know that?" I asked.

"Because his teeth are ground almost flat," Sam said.

He started stroking Toby between his ears, and Toby scrunched down, settling into Sam's lap.

"He looks like a mixture of a toy poodle and a Scottie, doesn't he?" Sam said, not speaking to me, but to the kid beside me.

"I think he looks like the Wizard of Oz dog," the kid said. "You know, Dorothy's dog, Toto?

"Right!" Sam said. "He does."

It was like I wasn't even there, like I was invisible.

Sam continued to scratch Toby's head between his ears, and Toby put his head back, sort of letting it loll to the side. I swear, if Toby had been a cat, he'd have been purring all over the place by then.

"Where'd you get him?" the kid said, turning to me.

Where? I didn't know. I'd just had him forever. I knew Elizabeth had gotten him when I was pretty little.

I turned Elizabeth. She was staring into the fire, her shoulders hunched, her elbows resting on her knees. "Where'd we get him, Elizabeth?" I asked.

"Who?"

"Toby! Where'd we get him?"

"How do I know?" she said.

I just shrugged and turned back.

The kid made a face, like, What's the matter with her?

I made a face back. I knew Elizabeth was strange. But it wasn't up to this kid to say so.

I could feel that aching in my head and throat again,

and I wanted to go to bed, but I couldn't leave Toby here.

"I'll take Toby now," I said, holding my hands out for him.

"Why don't you bring Toby a bed from the barn?" Sam said, still not addressing me, and making no move to hand Toby back to me, either. "Your dad has extra bedding out in the barn, doesn't he, Nick? Or maybe back at your house?"

Nick!?

I turned to look at the kid. A boy? Really? But he was . . . cute . . . or good-looking or something. Really a boy?

I suppose if he took his hat off we could tell better. Didn't anyone ever tell him he shouldn't wear a hat in the house?

"Yeah, my pa's got extras of everything," the kid said — I mean Nick said. "We had that nice bed for Elmo, remember? I think it's in our cellar. I could air it out and bring it in. It'll only take a minute."

"And when you do, Nicholas," Maura spoke up softly. "Clean up those boots first, all right?"

It seemed that all of us looked at Nick's feet then — even Elizabeth seemed to come out of her daze.

There was mud not only on his boots but all over the floor, too.

"Oops," Nick said. "Sorry. I'll clean it up."

He grinned at Maura, and she smiled back.

Funny, but I felt . . . what? Jealous, maybe? How could I be jealous of people I didn't even know?

"Now," Maura said, turning to me, "I think we should tuck you in bed."

"You sick?" Nick said, sticking his face up close to mine again. "What's the matter with you?"

What business was that of his?

I didn't see any way not to answer, though, not without being rude. "I have a cold," I said, and I deliberately breathed heavily, blowing my breath right in his face. "A *bad* cold."

He didn't back away, though, as if he hadn't even noticed. "Want me to take care of Toto while you're in bed?" he said.

"It's not *Toto*, it's *Toby!*" I said. "And no, I don't want you to take care of him!" I held out my hands to Sam. "Can I have my dog back now, please?" I said.

Sam lifted Toby gently and handed him back to me. "A nice dog," he said quietly.

"Thanks," I said.

"You staying here?" Nick asked me.

I nodded.

"You know how to ride?" he said.

" 'Course!" I said. "I've been riding since I was three!"

"I been riding since I was two!" Nick said. "Maybe you and me can ride someday. Me and Pa take care of the horses here. Our house is right out back."

Oh. That kind of *ride*. As in *ride horses*. I'd never been on a horse in my life — well, except for a pony ride when I was a kid. I'd been thinking bikes! But I sure wasn't going to correct that now.

"Want to?" Nick said.

"Maybe," I said.

"We got good trails. I could show you foxes and stuff. This time of year, the elk herds move. We could try and see some. Tomorrow?"

I shook my head. "I don't feel good. I told you that."

"Day after?" Nick said.

I shrugged.

"Nicholas," Maura said softly. "Nicholas, let her be. Let her get settled, first."

"Yeah," I said. "I should get settled first."

For a long minute, Nick just looked at me, his arms folded. "You scared?" he said.

"Scared of what?" I said, and I glared back at him over Toby's head.

"Horses," he said.

"Oh, right," I said, real sarcastically.

I saw Sam looking at me then, a little half-smile on his face, as if he was wondering too if I was scared.

Why were they both bugging me?

"I might ride day after tomorrow," I said, turning and looking out the window, as though I was studying the hills and trails out there. "But mostly, I like to ride by myself. Anyway you'll probably be in school. Or something."

"Something," Maura said. "Yes, something, but probably not school." Her tone was light, but I could tell she was serious.

"I go most of the time!" Nick said.

"Now, do you really?" Maura said.

"Well, my pa says I don't have to go every single teeny-weeny day."

"But perhaps a couple of teeny-weeny days a year wouldn't hurt you?" Maura said.

There was a moment of silence and then Nick said, "I went. One teeny day."

Suddenly, they all burst out laughing — Nick, Sam, and Maura, too.

Nick turned to me then, grinning, as if he had just gotten away with something. "How long you staying?" he asked.

Again I looked at Elizabeth, but again she wasn't looking back.

Sam looked at her, too.

"Don't know," I said.

I waited to see if Elizabeth would add anything, but she didn't.

So I just gave the best answer I could. "A while," I said. "We're staying for a while."

And I assumed that that, at least, was true.

Chapter 10

Maura showed me to a room upstairs at the back of the house, and I lay down there and stayed there for days, too sick to get up, too sick to care about anything but sleeping.

Elizabeth came and fussed over me, bringing me ginger ale and aspirin, and when I started to feel a little better, some soft-boiled eggs and toast and tea. But then she got sick, too, got whatever it was I had, and then Maura took over caring for me.

I've never had trays like Maura brought then — trays all prettied up with flowers and lace-trimmed napkins. Once, when I was just too tired to feed myself, she fed me tiny sips of soup from a spoon until I had swallowed the whole thing.

All that while, I was thinking of Sam and about my dream of staying here. But now the dream was different — changed — confused. When I was awake, I kept puzzling at it, and when I was asleep, I dreamed about it. In my dreams, I was waving good-bye to Elizabeth, but when I turned back, the whole house and ranch were gone, even Toby was gone, and I was standing there in the dark, calling for someone, and all I heard was my own voice echoing, as if I was in a canyon.

Then I'd wake up, sweating, knowing it was just a dream, a fever dream.

I knew that when I began to feel better, I'd figure it out. But I was just too tired and maybe too sick to try to figure it out right then.

Sometimes when I woke up, Toby was sleeping right on my bed; other times he was gone. But I guess he was getting along all right with the other dogs because I'd see him bound in and out of my room, not at all afraid.

Once I woke up and Nick was standing at the foot of my bed, staring at me, but when he saw that I was awake, he just disappeared without a word.

I don't know how many days I had been sick — maybe just three or four, maybe more, when I woke up one morning and knew that I felt well enough to get up. I took off the nightgown I had been sleeping in, one Maura had brought me, long, and warm, big enough for two people, practically. I found my jeans and T-shirt and socks that were on a chair by the bed, the same ones I had been wearing when I got here, although they looked to me to have been washed and folded. But when I put them on, the jeans felt huge around the waist. Man! I must have been sick a long time — I'd lost a lot of weight.

After I was dressed, I went out in the hall, hiking up my jeans. I looked around, saw a back stairs that twisted around alongside a wall, and started down it. I was going to go explore, see what I could see before anyone saw me. But I was only halfway down the stairs when I met Maura coming out of a small room on the landing.

Her face lit up in that sweet smile she has, as though she was genuinely happy to see me. "I'm glad to see you feeling better, lamb!" she said. "Wobbly still?"

I nodded. "A little."

She looked me up and down. "Is that all the clothes you have to put on?" she said. "You'll catch your death in that."

I folded my arms across me and could feel my jeans slip down on my hips. "I have clothes," I said, snatching at my jeans and rolling the top over to make them tighter. "I don't know where my suitcase is, though."

"I put it in your closet," Maura said, "but I have some fine, warm things right here for you. Follow me."

She went back into the small room that she had just come from. It looked like a huge walk-in linen closet — shelves piled high with blankets and pillows and folded clothes, a pile of sheets dumped in the middle of the room as though someone had just stripped a bed, some sweaters drying on a rack set up over the radiator.

"Here!" she said. "There must be something in here to fit you."

She went to a shelf in a far corner and lifted off a stack of folded sweaters and sweatshirts. There must have been thirty of them there, more sweaters than I had probably owned in my whole entire life. She set the stack down in front of me. "Look through these and take any you want."

I unfolded the top one — a gray sweatshirt with the words UNIVERSITY OF COLORADO across the front. It was enormous, probably big enough to fit Maura, and soft, too, and I knew it would be warm.

"Can I borrow this?" I asked.

"You can have it."

"Is it yours?"

"It's yours now."

"I'll give it back."

She didn't argue. She just watched while I slid the shirt on, and when my head came out on the other side, she reached over and smoothed it down over me.

"Better?" she said.

I nodded. I felt like I used to when I was a little kid playing dress-up, it was so huge. But it was warm.

"Now you go to the kitchen and get yourself some food. It's right at the bottom of these stairs. You help yourself to anything you'd like. I'll be there by and by to keep you company."

She switched off the light in the little room, and we both went out onto the landing.

I paused for a moment, because I wanted to say

thank you to her, not just for the sweatshirt, but for being so nice to me while I was sick. But when I started to speak, I couldn't think how to say it, and ended up saying something stupid. "I'm okay now," I said, and I turned away, embarrassed or shy or something.

"You are okay, lamb," Maura answered. "And don't you worry about anything from here on in. Everything's going to be all right, especially now that you're better."

"Is Elizabeth better, too?" I asked.

"Much," Maura said. "She left early this morning."

I whirled around, my heart suddenly racing. "Left?"

"Just for the day, lamb. She'll be back tonight."

"Where did she go?" I asked.

"Checking out some art school or art supply place or something, she said," Maura answered. "But don't worry, she'll be back tonight."

I nodded and turned away again, trying not to let show what I was feeling. Knowing Elizabeth, she could just as easily be gone for a while. She wouldn't mean to, but she'd get sidetracked.

I couldn't believe how hard my heart was thumping suddenly.

I found the kitchen at the foot of the stairs, just like Maura had said, and for a moment — just a moment — forgot Elizabeth completely. Here was another room to fall in love with.

It was a big room, painted yellow, the ceiling so high you couldn't even reach to the top of the top cabinets without a ladder or a step stool. The cabinets were painted white, and there was one huge floor-to-ceiling window that let in lots of light, and there were some stringy geraniums climbing up the windowpanes. There was a big silver stove and more plants in a corner and a rocking chair. It was all so nice, like pictures in books of what a grandma's kitchen should look like.

I let it all sink in for a while, then went to the refrigerator and got out some milk and orange juice and butter. Then I found cereal and bread, and I learned how to work the toaster, a weird toaster where the sides opened out, and you had to turn the toast over when it was half done, or else one side got all toasted and the other side stayed plain.

I got all my food together, the toast and all, and took it to the table and put it there. It was a room I felt I could stay in happily for a long time, just the way I'd felt about the library room that first day. But I didn't want to stay here alone. I wanted Elizabeth to come back to me. I knew she would, but I prayed that it would be soon — today.

I sat down and was just starting to eat when the kitchen door swung inward and the big Labs came in, one following the other, head to heel, with Toby trotting happily behind.

All three of them came right over to me at the table.

Were the big dogs going to be mad at me for being here?

They didn't seem to be. They weren't growling or worrying at me, just sniffing, their soft noses going back and forth. Breakfast time, they seemed to say, and they put their heads into my lap, one on either side.

Toby only came up to my ankle practically, but he was nudging me, so I picked him up and hugged him. "I've missed you," I whispered.

He snuffled some and licked my ear, and then I set him back on the floor.

He went and lay down in a little circular basket by the stove, probably the bed Nick had brought in from the barn. It was just his size. Beside it were two enormous beds like huge, crumpled nests — the Labs' beds.

I broke off a piece of toast and held it out to the boy dog. He took it carefully, as though he didn't want to hurt my hand. The other dog sniffed and made a little sound, almost like a little humming in her throat, and turned and walked right into the leg of the table.

"Silly dog," I said. I reached down and gave her the other piece.

She took it from my hand, crossed the room with it in her mouth, and walked smack into a cabinet.

"Hey, dumb dog!" I said. "Pay attention to where you're going."

She lay down, the toast between her front paws.

I got up to make myself more toast, the boy dog following me, just as Maura came in.

"These two big bums found you, huh?" she said.

"What are their names?" I asked.

"This big guy here is Monte," she said, fondling the head of the boy dog. "And that one, the blind one, that's his mother, Cody."

"She's blind? How come? What happened to her?"

"We don't know. It happened last summer. Several other dogs in the neighborhood went blind, too. The vet thinks it was some kind of virus. But she does okay, don't you, Cody?"

Cody had come to Maura and lay her head against Maura's leg, nudging with her head, begging to be petted. "You're a fine one, aren't you?" Maura said, bending down and patting her.

Cody nudged some more, hard.

Maura laughed, then moved over and settled herself into the rocking chair, Cody following. I swear, Cody looked like she wanted to climb into Maura's lap, the way she kept nudging and pushing.

"Now, then," Maura said to me, after she was settled in the chair, Cody's head in her lap. "You had enough to eat? Do you feel better? And warmer?"

I nodded. "Better. And warmer."

"Would you like to see some of the ranch today?" she asked. "*Not* from horseback?" She was smiling when she said that.

Was she telling me that she knew I couldn't ride?

But all I said was, "Who with?"

"Me. Me and your grandfather."

"Oh," I said.

Maura just smiled.

There was silence for a while, and then Maura said, "He's a good man, your grandfather."

What could I say to that? I didn't know whether he was a good man or not. All I knew was that he was mad at Elizabeth and he hadn't liked my dad. Still, I didn't want to hurt her feelings, because she is married to him, so I didn't say anything.

"His bark is worse than his bite," Maura went on, as if she knew what I was thinking. "He means nothing by it."

I still didn't know how to answer that, so I still didn't say anything. But I waited, wondering if she'd say more.

"They're too much alike, he and your mama," Maura went on. "That's why they don't get along. They can be hateful together. One at a time, they're good enough folks."

How did she know that about Elizabeth?

"So give him a chance, lamb," Maura said. "He shouldn't have said some of the things he said, scolding your mama like that in front of you, saying mean things about your poor pa — God rest his soul — but that's his way. He's probably sorry by now, but he'd never say so."

It wouldn't matter if he did say so. How come people don't understand that? If you say something, you've said it. Saying "I'm sorry" afterward doesn't change it.

"Please come with us, lamb? He wants to check

some fences and see to the cattle, where they are, all that, before winter sets in. You'll like it."

How come people always think they know what other people will like? But then, if I didn't go, I'd probably just spend all day looking out the window, watching for Elizabeth and worrying and stuff.

"Can the dogs come?" I asked.

Maura laughed. "Try and stop them. They come everywhere with us."

"How long will we be?"

"Two, three hours." She smiled. "You can stand it that long."

Maybe. "I'll clean up my dishes," I said. "Then I'll be ready."

"And I'll have a little tea while you do that," Maura said. She gave Cody's head a little push away, then went to the stove and put the kettle on to boil, while I went and washed and dried the dishes. The plates were pretty — blue with pink edges, and the bowls were pink with blue edges.

Elizabeth and I don't own any dishes as pretty as these — well, we don't own much of anything but clothes and a few books and stuff. It must be nice to be able to buy things for your table, knowing you'll have a table next week — and knowing where it will be.

Where would we be next week? Here? Or somewhere else? And where was Elizabeth right now?

I sighed and reached up to the cabinet to put away the plates.

"I wouldn't worry too much," Maura said softly.

"I'm not worried," I said. But then, without turning around, I added, "When did she leave?"

"Early — about seven o'clock. But she'll be back."

I wiped and dried the last plate, then hung up the dish towel very straight. This was the kind of room you had to leave neat and clean, not because it was a fussy room, but because it wasn't. But it needed to be left nice for when you came back.

Would Elizabeth be back? She'd never leave me, not for good, I knew I could count on that. Then I had this terrible sneaky thought that I immediately pushed away: did I even want her back? But of course I did. Still, knowing her, I knew better than Maura did that I might or might not be able to count on her for tonight.

Chapter 11

We all piled into the jeep — Maura, Sam, me, and the three dogs. The Labs jumped right in, Cody not even bumping her head. I had to lift Toby up, though, because even though he kept leaping, then backing up and leaping again, he just couldn't make it with those stubby little legs.

I got him in, hugged him, then settled in the backseat with all the dogs while Maura took the wheel, Sam beside her. Sam was wrapped in a huge sheepskin coat that hung down over his knees and came all the way up around his skinny neck to cover his ears. Seeing him wrapped that way, I couldn't help thinking of those pictures in my old fairy tale book of Old Man Winter with his frosty breath, all wrapped in furs. This one wasn't a nice fairy tale person, though, at least not that day. He'd been grumpy ever since he got in the car, complaining about everything from the weather to the smell of the dogs to the aching in his knees.

We had just settled in and were closing the car door when Nicholas appeared, running up alongside the car.

"Hey, wait up!" he shouted. "Where you going?"

Sam rolled down his window. "Looking things over," he said. "Come on. Pile in!"

"Nah!" Nick, said, but he leapt up onto the side step of the jeep. "I'm going to ride. Tanya needs exercise, Pa says."

Tanya? A horse named Tanya?

Nick leaned in the window. "You better?" he said to me.

"Sort of," I said. And then, to head him off, I added, "Not well enough to ride yet, though." And I felt proud of myself for just saying *ride*, as in *ride horses*.

Nick grinned. "See you later," he said, and he jumped back off.

Sam turned his head and watched until Nick disappeared behind the barn. With Sam turned that way, I could see the look on his face — soft, almost tender, the way I had seen Mr. Ogden look at Michael and Jason sometimes.

Funny. Sam obviously wasn't Nick's father. But then I wondered: can you feel fatherly toward someone even if you're not his father?

Maura started up the car then, and we bounced off down the drive, then off onto another road, as bumpy as the one Elizabeth and I had come in on. The dogs kept sliding over, crowding me all the way over to the far door, and I had to keep shifting them back.

As we drove, every little while, Sam would begin to cough. He would cough so much you would just think that he was about to die right on the spot, the way he fought for breath.

Maura wouldn't say anything then, but I could tell by the back of her neck and her shoulders how tense she was, as if she was waiting for his breath to come back before she could start breathing again for herself. Did he always cough like this? Or had he gotten the same flu Elizabeth and I had had?

We drove awhile, none of us talking much, all of us, even the dogs, just looking out the windows. Well, Cody didn't look out. She just sat there seeing nothing, so I wrapped an arm around her neck and hugged her, so she could feel someone was with her, even if she couldn't see.

Once, we saw a whole herd of horses — wild ones, Maura said they were. They were far away, and the closer we came, the faster they ran. They didn't seem afraid, just like they were playing. Watching them play like that, rear up high, just the way horses do in movies, made me think that God had put them down here so he'd have someone to play with and he wouldn't be lonely.

But I guess God is never lonely, because he can make his own friends for himself — mothers and kids and grandfathers, too.

Was there really something to this God story the

nuns had told us? These mountains and trees and valleys! Could this whole place just have spun out from one little dust explosion or something? Well, maybe it could — what did I know? But it seemed easier in my mind to believe that it was created. And created so different from back home, too. We just don't have mountains and spaces like this.

I began to think that Maura and Sam weren't really checking the fences and the cattle, because we never stopped to get out, never made notes about broken fences or anything. I think Sam was just too old and sick to do anything else, so Maura drove him around so he'd feel important, king of his ranch. I couldn't blame him for that, though. I guess I'd feel important, too, if I owned this place, if I could ride around thinking, This is mine. This is all mine.

We had been driving maybe an hour, just bouncing along trails, saying things like, "Look at that," or "What's that?" or "Isn't that pretty?" when Maura said to me, over her shoulder, "So what do you think, lamb? Pretty enough for you?"

"It's beautiful," I said. "Really, really beautiful."

Sam swiveled around to face me. "You really like it?" he asked.

"Yes," I answered. "I love it."

He looked at me for a long time, and then beyond me and out the window. His eyes were soft, almost the same look as when he had watched Nick before. After a while, he said quietly, "I do, too. I love this land."

Loves it more than he loves people, Elizabeth had said once.

But I didn't say that out loud.

Sam looked back at me. "Are you always this quiet?" he asked. It wasn't mean the way he said it, just as though he was curious.

I shook my head. "No," I said. "It's just that this place . . . I don't know. I guess it makes you think."

Sam nodded slowly, and for the first time that day, he smiled. "Yes," he said, "it makes you think. The mountains, the —"

"Horses!" I said suddenly. "It's the horses I was thinking about. It's like one day God needed a place for horses to live . . ."

I stopped, embarrassed, could feel my face get flaming hot.

I turned and looked out the window. I couldn't believe I'd said that, not to him! I must have sounded like a complete jerk.

Sam began coughing then. He turned back front and coughed and coughed. It wasn't one of those can't-breathe coughs, though. It was over quickly, and for a second, I even wondered if he had faked it — faked it to help cover my embarrassment?

No, he wasn't kind like that, I didn't think.

When he had stopped coughing, Maura said to me, "Want to see more, lamb?" She had turned her head slightly to look at me. "Or do you want to turn back?"

"What're you asking her for?" Sam said, his usual, grumpy tone back again. "Why don't you ask me?"

110

Spoiled grouch.

"Do you want to keep going?" she asked the grouch.

"Yes," he said.

"Okay with you, lamb?" she said over her shoulder.

For a moment, I felt like saying no, just to be spiteful to him. But that would have meant that Maura would have had to decide between him and me, and that wouldn't be fair to her. "It's okay with me," I said.

So we drove some more. There weren't any roads, just tracks kind of, like paths that ran through the mountains and along fields, where there were zillions of cows, and down into valleys between trees that hung low all around us. Each part of this ranch was prettier than the last.

"So you really like it, huh?" Sam said to me over his shoulder.

I'd already said I did, said I loved it. But since he seemed to need to hear it again, I said, "I like it lots."

"Your ma hates it."

What was I supposed to say to that?

Maura said, "There, now," to him, and I saw over the seat that she put a hand on his bony knee.

"Well, she does. All this I built up, and she spits on it, that's what she does, spits on it." He began coughing again, a real-sounding cough this time.

I bet she didn't spit on it, not ever. I've lived with Elizabeth for eleven years and not even once have I seen her spit. I was going to tell him that, but he was coughing so hard I had to wait to see if he was going to die first.

When he finally stopped coughing, I surprised myself by saying, "You don't like her much, do you?"

He pretended not to hear, but from the way his ears
got red, I knew he had.

"He likes her well enough, lamb," Maura said.

He swiveled in his seat to face me again. "Do you
like her?" he asked.

"Do I like her?" I said.

"Yes, you. Do you like your mother?"

What a question!

"I . . . well, yeah, I guess. I mean, of course. She's
my mother."

"And she's my daughter."

"So?" I said.

"So you're no dumbbell," he said. "I could tell that
the first time I laid eyes on you. Not much to look at
maybe, but you're not dumb, either. You know what
I'm talking about. Just because she's your mother, you
don't have to like her. And just because she's my
daughter, doesn't mean I have to like her, either. I
guess I . . . well, I do . . . I love her. But she sure is
difficult."

I just stared at him. How could he say things like
that, about his own daughter?

But how did I honestly feel about her? I loved her —
just like he had said. But he was right — she is difficult.

"Now, see them?" Sam said. He pointed to a steep
hillside where four — no, five — horses were gallop-

ing, chasing each other, it looked like. They couldn't have been wild horses, because there was a fence around the hillside.

"See them there?" he said. "Some of the best, most expensive breeding horses in the world. There's only nine of that kind that exist. I own five of them."

"That's nice," I said.

"*Nice?* Each of them is worth a fortune. Probably more money for *each* of those horses than you or your mother have seen in your entire life."

And you're bragging about that?

As though he was reading my mind, he said, "I'm bragging." He was quiet for a moment, and then he sighed deeply. "I shouldn't," he said softly. "Because it's not what I own that's important." He turned to Maura. "You know that, don't you? It's the land I love."

"I know that," she said. "I know."

"Land that I love," he repeated quietly. "Yet her mother hates it, hates all of it, or says she does. Although maybe it's just me she can't stand. Now, you . . ." He patted her hand on the steering wheel.

"It's all right, now," she said soothingly. "It's all right. To each his own." She patted his hand back.

Again, I heard him sigh deeply, and Maura patted him some more.

I felt sad for him then. Clearly he loved this place, and he wanted so much for Elizabeth to love it, too. But you can't make people love things just because you do. I already knew that. How come he didn't? Elizabeth didn't care about most of the things I cared about — a home, friends. Maura was right: to each his own.

For Sam, at least, he had his own: Maura, his land.

For me, I wondered if anyplace, anybody, would ever feel like my own.

Chapter 12

Elizabeth didn't come home that night, but when it was very late, about ten o'clock, she did call. She'd be back next day, she said, but was staying in town because there was so much to do and to check out at that art school. Before she hung up, she gave me the number of the motel where she was staying.

As soon as we said good-bye, I called the number back. I asked for her, and the person at the desk rang her room.

I didn't wait for her to pick up, though, didn't want her to know I was checking up on her. I just wanted to be sure she was where she'd said she was.

The next morning, I was in the kitchen having breakfast when Nick appeared. He was wearing his heavy, muddy boots and a wool jacket and that weird hat that hid his hair. The dogs were trailing behind him, Toby, too.

And why did that make me mad?

I called Toby over and picked him up, holding him close to me.

Toby let me hug him for a minute, but then struggled to get away. Gently, I set him back on the floor.

Right away, he went over to the other dogs, who had settled by Nick's dirty, muddy feet.

"You better take those boots off," I said.

Nick just shrugged, then reached down and began patting Toby, kind of absentmindedly.

"Want to ride today?" he asked, looking up at me.

I couldn't think of an excuse, so I just said, "Maybe." I'd figure out an excuse later. But then I thought, Maybe I won't make up an excuse. I've always wanted to ride — if I could just do it without looking like an idiot.

"I saw elk yesterday," Nick said. "A whole herd."

"Elk aren't the same as deer, right?" I said.

"Nope. Different. Lots bigger. Kind of scary up close, they're so big. Ever seen one?"

I shook my head. "I live in a city," I said.

"What's it like, the city?" Nick asked.

I shrugged. "Regular. It's okay. Mine isn't a real city kind of city, though, more like suburbs. But we don't have wildlife, unless you count squirrels." I laughed, remembering. "And pigeons," I added.

"Foxes?" he asked.

"Of course not!"

"Why not?"

"I told you! 'Cause it's a city!"

"We have lots of foxes," Nick said. "That's why we have llamas."

"What do llamas have to do with foxes?"

He rolled up his eyes. "Llamas chase foxes, bird-brain! A good llama can outrun even a fast fox, can keep them away from the sheep and stuff."

He was still scratching Toby's head and Toby rolled over on his side, then on his back, paws in the air — and I was getting mad. I knew it was stupid, but I couldn't help it. It felt like he was taking over my dog.

"Is it true there aren't any stars in cities?" Nick went on, looking up at me.

"Of course there are stars, birdbrain!" I answered.

Nick shrugged, and I thought he was blushing. "I heard there weren't," he said, and he looked away.

"Well, there are," I answered. And because I felt bad for adding the birdbrain part, I added, "It's just that they're harder to see because of the lights."

"So, want to ride today?" he asked again. He stood up, and Toby scrambled to his feet, too.

I started to say no, but then I thought, What else would I do all day? The day before, I'd been bored after we got back from seeing the ranch, even though I'd taken a long, long walk by myself. And I did want to try it.

I shrugged. "Maybe."

"Meet you out by the barn?" he said.

"I have to clean up first," I said, and I looked at my dishes, but I was also thinking of the floor, the mud he had tracked in. It wasn't nice to Maura to make a mess like that.

He didn't answer, just went out, holding the door while all the dogs — Toby, too — followed him.

"Traitor!" I whispered after Toby.

After I had cleaned up my dishes *and* the mud, I went upstairs and put on some warm things — sneakers and heavy socks, my warmest jeans, and a big sweater with Maura's sweatshirt on top. It had gotten very cold out, and the day before, I'd almost frozen when I'd gone out for my walk.

I couldn't find any mittens — they were probably still packed with my winter things somewhere in the car. So I went into Elizabeth's room, found a pair of her gloves, and put them on.

I wouldn't lose them.

Then I went outside — around back and down to the barn.

I was nervous, but not really scared. I had ridden a horse once, at one of those country fairs, round and round a ring. It hadn't been that hard, I remembered.

It wasn't a very long walk to the barn, but the wind had come up and it was even colder than the day before, really cold for September — at least for September back home. Maybe it was always this cold here in September.

I got to the barn just as Nick appeared, leading an enormous black horse, its stirrups or reins or whatever jangling.

The horse was huge! I hoped it was Nick's horse, not mine!

I'd started to take a wide detour around them when Nick called to me. "Here! Hold him!" he said. "I'm going back for Tanya."

"Hold him?" I said.

"Yeah. Just hold his reins, I'll be right back. I need to saddle up Tanya." He patted the huge rump of the horse I was suddenly holding. "I did Buddy here for you."

Buddy? Tyrannosaurus rex would be more like it.

I held tight to the reins — at least I knew what they were, *reins* and *stirrups* being the only horse words I knew. My heart was beating like crazy as Nick disappeared into the barn, leaving me alone with this huge creature.

I could already tell that it didn't like me, the way it kept looking at me out of the corners of its wild-looking eyes.

Do horses bite?

"Nice horse," I whispered. "Nice horsie."

Suddenly he shook all over, his fur or hide or whatever rippling from his head right down to his tail. He shook so hard he almost pulled the reins out of my hands.

I started to yell, "Hey, cut that out!" But then I thought better of it, so I just said softly, "I'd rather if you didn't do that, okay?"

That's when he laughed at me. His big black lips

quivered, and his breath came out in a cloud of steam while he snorted. Loud.

Nick appeared then, leading his horse, a horse even bigger than Buddy.

Jeez! I had no idea horses were so big. The one at the fair that time must have been just a baby.

"Ready?" Nick said. "Let's go."

In one smooth movement, he swung one leg into the stirrup, the other over the horse, and was on.

Man! I'd never be able to do that.

Once he was up there, he frowned down at me. "Hey, birdbrain!" he said. "You going to ride that way?"

"What way?" I said. "I'm going to get *on* the horse, if that's what you mean!"

"I meant in sneakers," he said.

I shrugged and looked down at my feet. "I left my riding shoes home."

"*Shoes?* You don't have boots?"

I shook my head.

"You must be a good rider," Nick said. "With sneakers, I can never keep my feet in the stirrups."

He shrugged. "Let's go. I'll show you the best trail."

He turned his horse, and I watched them trot away, his horse looking even bigger from behind.

I almost shouted, "Don't go!" but bit it back.

Oh, well. This couldn't be too hard. If I could just figure out how to get on.

I put one foot in the stirrup and started to hoist myself off the ground.

Nope, wrong foot. I had put in the near foot. You had to put in the *far* foot, so you could swing over with the other one.

I had just repositioned, was just about to do it right, when stupid Buddy moved.

"Hold it!" I said. But he didn't. He tossed his head back and forth, back and forth. "Stop!"

He pulled so hard that the reins slid from my hands, and he began to trot away . . . with one of my feet still in his stirrup.

I screamed, terrified, but at the same moment, my foot slipped out.

I was now on my butt on the ground and Buddy was running free.

"Hey!" I heard Nick yell.

I saw him turn Tanya around and go galloping after my runaway horse.

Oh, jeez, now I was in trouble. What if he couldn't catch him?

I picked myself up and dusted off my seat, watching Nick try to round up Buddy. Nick really *was* a cowboy. It took him only a minute to do it. He raced up alongside my horse and reached out and caught the reins, all the while hanging onto his own horse. When he had Buddy's reins secured, he turned both horses around and headed back to me, Buddy trotting alongside.

Nick wasn't even breathing hard. Buddy, though, was blowing out his breath, making those huffy horse noises, and I just knew he was laughing at me again.

Stupid horse!

I watched them come to me, trying to think what to say about why Buddy had escaped.

"What happened?" Nick said. He leaned down and tried to hand me back the reins.

But I backed away, my hands in my pockets, "Can't," I said. I swallowed, then said what I knew I had to say. But I said it so fast it came out like one word. "I've-never-been-on-a-horse-before," I said.

"What?" Nick said.

I backed away some more. "I *said!*" I repeated, mad-like, "I've. Never. Been. On. A. Horse. Before. Okay?" I said it real deliberately as if he was hard of hearing. "Not a real horse, anyway," I added.

"But you said you've been riding since —"

"So I lied!" I said. "Okay?"

"Birdbrain!" Nick said.

"Birdbrain!" I shot back.

He glared at me and I glared back.

"Jeez!" he muttered.

For a minute, neither of us said anything more. Then suddenly Nick jumped down from his horse and linked her reins over a fence post with one hand, still holding Buddy's reins in the other hand. He came over to me then, Buddy following behind like a regular, well-behaved horse.

I was backing away again.

"Come on," Nick said. "I'll show you how to do it."

He slid Buddy's reins over another fence post, then

122

folded both his hands together and held them out to me, like for a boost.

I looked at him doubtfully.

"You'll do all right," he said. "We'll go slow."

"What if he runs away with me?"

"He won't."

I took a deep breath, put one foot into his hands, and took his lift up, swinging my other foot over Buddy's back.

God! It was high up there.

I grabbed tight to the saddle knob.

Nick handed up the reins to me, but I couldn't take them. Both my hands were firmly around that knob.

"Come on, you can do it," Nick said. "Hold these in one hand." He uncurled one of my fists from around the saddle thing and made me take the reins. "It's like this: pull to the right if you want him to go right, left for left, and back, to your stomach, to make him stop. To make him go, kick him. Hard."

"Oh, right," I muttered.

"Right!" Nick said enthusiastically.

Obviously, sarcasm was lost on him.

"Just remember to pull back on the reins to stop," he said. "That's all you need to know."

"What if he doesn't listen?" I said.

"He will," Nick said.

He leapt up onto Tanya's back, bent over and released her reins from the post, then trotted up alongside me.

He smiled at me then, and I couldn't help smiling back. I was feeling better. Scared, but it really did feel good up there.

"Let's go," he said. "Just try to feel your horse and move with him."

Oh, right. When all I could think about was how to not fall off.

Nick moved away slowly, and right away, Buddy followed. Good thing, because I sure wouldn't have kicked him.

We just moved along together, Nick and Tanya, Buddy and me — me bumping a little in the saddle, Buddy swaying gently back and forth. We were going very slowly, the horses just walking.

I smiled and looked around.

I couldn't believe how good I felt suddenly, high above the ground.

We headed down a small hill, the horses still just walking slowly. I noticed, though, that while I was bumping up and down in the saddle, up in front of me, on Tanya, Nick wasn't. He was like glued to Tanya's back, moving smoothly with her.

He turned then and looked at me. "You're doing okay," he said. "Just try to feel Buddy's moves."

Try not to fall off, you mean!

We went through a grove of trees, the branches hanging so low that I had to duck to keep from bumping my head. At the foot of the hill was a shallow, rocky stream that our horses splashed through, speeding up once they got to the center, as though they wanted to get it over with in a hurry. Once across, the horses slowed to a walk again and we began heading upward, making our way slowly along a trail that ran along the very edge of a long slope. We went a long way, the trail narrow and rocky, and when I looked down once, I was suddenly terrified. We had come so far, were up so high, with no fences, no nothing between us and the edge of a ravine. Buddy seemed assured, though, as if he knew exactly where to step, and beneath me, I could hear the confident sound of his feet: *clop-clop, clop-clop*.

Only once did he stumble, and I felt myself slide sideways in the saddle. By the time I could pull back on the reins, though, he had righted himself and we were moving smoothly along again.

Up, up, up we climbed.

After a long time we paused and Nick pointed. Ahead of us, across the ravine, were deer, about a dozen of them who had come to a pond to drink. As we watched, right over their heads, a flock of ducks approached low, also heading for the pond. The ducks squawked and yammered, scolding the deer, but the deer didn't even bother to look up.

The ducks were heavy-bodied and clumsy as they came in for their landing, tilting awkwardly side to side, feet outstretched. On landing, they seemed to almost crash into the water. Yet once down, they were graceful, swimming in tight circles around each other, staying well out in the water away from the deer.

And all the while, the deer drank, unbothered by the ducks, unbothered by Nick and me.

After a while, Nick and I continued on. We weren't trotting or anything, still just walking our horses. I felt grateful to Nick for doing that, for not scaring me or embarrassing me or anything by going too fast. I also began trying out what Nick had said — practicing how to move with Buddy, to feel his motion — but I found it was awfully hard to do.

At the top of the next rise, we stopped again. This time, I saw the animal first. It was a fox, the first time I had seen one, other than in a zoo. Its tail was curled with a little white tip on the end, its body low-slung, reddish brown, not much different from a dog.

It had crept out from a hollow, and when it saw us, it disappeared as quickly as it had come. Only a branch quivering showed that anything had been there.

Again, Nick and I went on. Mountains just seemed to unfold before us, the peaks white with snow, or else brown, or even some that were still green. A hawk hung on a breeze, and I wondered briefly if it was the same hawk I had spotted the day I saw the deer. The silence was just incredible. It seemed there were no sounds at all until we stopped the horses and listened carefully. Then we could hear a world of sounds. Our horses breathing. A bird calling. Something rustling in the thicket. The sighing of the wind. The rustle of air made by geese or ducks as they winged by.

Occasionally, Nick looked back at me, but he didn't

break the silence. He would just nod, seeming satisfied that Buddy and I were okay.

Okay? I was more than okay — much, much more. How can I even say how I felt? Awesome. High on a horse, high on a hill.

And I couldn't help smiling suddenly, thinking of Sam's words: "It's the land I love."

Chapter 13

For the whole next week, Nick and I spent every possible waking minute on our horses, riding over that countryside, seeing everything. And there was so much to see, to learn. I began being able to identify trees, and I even learned the names of some of the mountains. I also learned from Nick about clouds, learned to recognize the signs that it was snowing on top of a particular peak. I saw prints of mountain lions, and saw lots of coyotes, close up, even. And I loved riding! Nick said he'd never seen anyone who had learned to ride so fast, that I was a natural.

Some natural! I fell off every time we went from trotting to galloping. I did get back on every time I fell, though, and it was only three times, really. I finally found that if I relaxed, wasn't tense and scared, I could fit with Buddy's strides, almost feeling his rhythm, just like Nick had said. And I found that if I thought

128

about it too much, then all the rhythm would be gone. It was really hard, and I wasn't good at it yet. But I was learning.

Every day we went out I learned more, too, and each day I got better. Nick and I would stuff some apples and crackers into our pockets for our lunch, and wouldn't get home till it was almost dark, and I'd be so exhausted I could barely stay awake to eat the late supper Maura had prepared for me in the kitchen.

Then next morning, we'd be up early and out early all over again.

My legs got sore from riding, and my bottom got really sore, and even my shoulders hurt. My ankles and calves especially ached from trying to keep my feet in the stirrups. I could see how boots would really help. Still, it was wonderful. To say that I loved this place wouldn't be saying anything. Yet I couldn't find the words to say it, couldn't find the words to say even to myself what it all meant to me. All I knew was I loved everything I saw, and it all made me want to see more.

I also liked being with Nick. He got on my nerves sometimes with his odd questions and know-it-all tone of voice and the way he kept getting in my face. But he was full of ideas, and I'd never met anybody else my age who was so . . . in charge, or something. He did practically anything he wanted and didn't do what he didn't want — like going to school. But he wasn't dumb. It was as though he was already all grown up, even though, like me, he was only eleven. I guess what I liked best was that in some ways we were a lot alike.

The only thing wrong was that Elizabeth still hadn't come back from town, where she was now going to that art school. She did call every night, did leave me messages if I wasn't there, and said for sure she'd be back on Saturday. Since she'd said there was no school on Saturday, I felt I could count on her for that at least. Still, I worried, and even felt guilty. I had been thinking of finding a home without her — and that seemed to be all right. Then why did it not feel all right to think that maybe she was deciding the same thing? Was it because it was all right for me to decide — but it was something else entirely to think that maybe I didn't have a choice? Yet if I did have a choice, what would I decide? Would I — could I — choose the ranch? Without her?

I was looking forward to seeing her, though, to telling her all about what I had found. I knew that the outdoors made her nervous, but I knew too that there were lots of things she'd love hearing about — like about the enormous jackrabbits we kept seeing, as big as small dogs they were, and the coyotes, and about the mouse nest we found at the base of a tree. And I couldn't wait to show her that I had learned to ride! Me. Me, who had never been on a horse in my life, now could ride.

I didn't think I'd tell her about the times I fell off,

though. I couldn't wait to saddle up Buddy and ride up to the house and see the look on her face.

On the Friday of that week, the day before she was coming home, when I came down early for breakfast, I found Maura in the kitchen with Nick, preparing a picnic lunch for us. She said if we insisted on being gone all day, she was going to be sure we had the right food.

She made a pretend mad face at me. "You'll be so thin you'll fit through a keyhole by the time your mother comes back," she said.

I smiled. "I think I've gotten fat," I said, and I showed her how my jeans were fitting snug around my waist again.

She just shook her head at me, but she was smiling.

Nick came and stood by me, giving me one of his close-up looks. I still didn't like the way he did that, but I was beginning to get used to it. I don't think he knew it was kind of rude.

"You're not fat *or* skinny," he said. "I think you're just right."

For some reason, I felt myself blushing like crazy, and I turned away from him and went to the stove.

I made myself a bowl of oatmeal and brought it to the table, where Maura was making the sandwiches. On the way, I stopped and patted Toby, who was curled up by the rocker. He opened one eye and then went right back to sleep.

Nick took one of Maura's sandwiches for his

breakfast and sat down with it, and I sat down across from him.

I had just started eating when Sam appeared, the first time I had ever seen him in the kitchen.

He had a huge box tucked under one arm, his cane hanging over the other. And he looked annoyed, his bushy black brows pulled tight together over his eyes.

"You two going to be gone all day again?" he said, mad-like.

I was surprised, hadn't thought he'd noticed what I did all day.

"You want to come, Mr. Carter?" Nick said, looking up from his plate.

I laughed, but Sam didn't. He just tilted his head, looking down at Nick from that height of his, as if he was thinking about it.

"You rode a lot this summer," Nick added.

Sam pulled his brows even tighter together. "I don't do well in the cold," he said. "These knees. Old bones ache, you know."

Nick just grinned. He has a really nice smile, with very white teeth, and a little gap between the two front ones. "So we'll come back if your old bones start hurting," he said.

Sam dropped the box on the table, then settled his long length into the chair next to Nick, and across from me. "Maybe another day," he said.

Maura smiled at him when he sat down and patted his hand.

He patted hers back, and that fierce look on his face was suddenly completely gone.

Funny, but for old people, they seemed to be in love.

It must be nice. I could see how he could love Maura, but I had a hard time with how she could love him. He made me nervous, maybe because he was always so grumpy.

"So, what are you finding on my ranch?" he said, looking across the table at me.

"Lots of things," I said.

"Like?"

"Like a fox the other day, the first one I've ever seen. And a bunch of ducks and geese. And this ravine, you should see it! There were deer across there, and —"

I stopped, feeling stupid. Of course he had seen the ravine. He owned it! I shrugged. "Well, I mean, I know you've seen it. But it was neat."

I took a bite of my oatmeal.

"We checked fences, too," Nick added.

"All okay?" Sam said.

Nick nodded. "What we saw was okay," he said.

"See any elk?" Sam asked.

Nick had just taken a huge bite of sandwich and struggled to speak around it.

I spoke for him. "No, but we saw tracks," I said.

"Where?" Sam said.

"Up near the peaks, where the snow is," I said.

"Nick says the elk have gone off up there. Hunting season is coming, so they leave. We're heading there today, and we're going to track them as far as we can."

"Amazing creatures, aren't they?" Maura said quietly. "I've often wondered how they know the season is coming. But every year they move out — before a shot is even fired."

"I bet they remember it from last year," I said.

Sam turned his fierce eyes on me. "How?" he said. It was abrupt, almost annoyed, the way he said it.

"How, what?" I said.

"How do you think they remember the exact time?" Sam said. "They couldn't know it before it comes."

I shrugged. "Maybe they could," I said. "Maybe they associate it with something, like how long the nights are, or how cold it is, or when the leaves have all fallen. Then when that happens, they know it's hunting time again."

"Nah, elk are too dumb for that," Nick said, in that superior voice that I hate.

But Sam was looking at me, his fierce eyebrows drawn together again — not mad, though, but more like he was thinking something. "You might be right," he said finally, nodding slowly. "I believe you might be onto something."

Pleased. I couldn't believe how pleased I felt. And for the second time that morning, I felt myself blushing.

"Nah," Nick said again. "Elk are dumb. Only people know that stuff."

"Don't overestimate human beings," Sam said, turning and pointing a finger at Nick. "And *never* underestimate an elk."

Sam turned back to me. "How about mountain lions? See any of them yet?"

I shook my head no. "I didn't," I said. "But Nick did. All I saw was the tail, disappearing behind the ash tree."

"The ash tree?" he asked.

I nodded. "You know, the one that's four hundred years old, Nick said."

"What'd you think of it?"

"Think? Man, I look at it and wonder, and I picture what might have happened under that tree. Do you realize, four hundred years ago, Indians might have been resting under there? Or maybe the settlers coming across in their wagons stopped there. Or —"

Jeez! I was mortified again. Why did I keep doing this with him — telling him about things I was thinking when I didn't even know I was thinking them?

I must have been weird. I never said things like this to anyone else, not even Elizabeth. It was just that this stuff seemed to spill out with him whenever we talked about this place — maybe because I knew how much he loved this land, too.

But one good thing about Sam — if he noticed I was embarrassed, he never showed it. He always seemed to know how to change the conversation or whatever.

He stood up abruptly, his cane in his right hand,

using his left as a lever to lift himself off his chair. Once up, he patted Maura again, then started for the door. But there, he stopped. "That box," he said, turning and pointing with the top of his cane at the box he'd left on the table. "It's for you."

Me? Was he talking to me? Or Nick?

I looked at the box, then back at him.

But he was already gone.

"It's yours," Maura said to me.

"Mine?" I said. "What is it?"

"I think you'll want to open it," she said, smiling.

Nick shoved the box across the table to me. "Hurry up!" he said.

I took the box and lifted the lid.

It wasn't sealed or anything, but the lid was hard to get off and I had to tug at it. When it finally did come off, all I could see underneath was a mass of tissue paper, crinkly and white. I took that out, and underneath was more paper, heavy, like packing paper.

"Let me see!" Nick said. He reached over, as though he was going to take the paper out himself.

"Out of here!" I said, pushing away his hands.

I lifted out the packing paper myself.

More paper underneath, shredded paper, the kind that dishes or glassware come wrapped in.

I lifted that out, too.

And under that — under that was a pair of boots, beautiful brown leather boots with decorations on them, carved into the leather. They had pointy toes like cowboy boots, and a tablike thing at the top for pulling them on, and a sort of high heel, perfect for keeping your feet in the stirrups.

Cowboy boots.

Riding boots.

Beautiful riding boots!

I lifted them out and held them up.

"Hey, cool!" Nick said.

More than cool.

I couldn't even speak.

I peeked inside to see if they were my size, but I couldn't see any markings.

I kicked off my sneakers, then bent and slid one foot into a boot. It was hard at first to get on, hard to slip over the arch of my foot.

But once it was on, I could tell it fit perfectly. Perfectly!

I did the other one, then stood up.

Nick had jumped up and come around the table. "Let me see!" he said. "Let's see you walk in them."

I walked halfway across the room, then turned back, grinning.

I was tall in them, too, with those high heels.

"Cool!" Nick said again. "Now we can gallop and everything!"

"Now, Nick!" Maura said warningly.

But I just laughed.

"Maura!" I said. "How did you know — he know — I needed them? How did you know my size?"

"I didn't," she said. "But you leave your sneakers inside the door every night. Your grandfather looked inside them for the size."

Your grandfather.

"But how did he know I needed them?" I said.

Maura just looked at me, smiling. She didn't answer, didn't have to answer that.

Because he did.

"Let's go!" Nick said. "You ready?"

Ready?

Not quite.

"In a minute," I said.

And I went out through the swinging doors to the library, where I knew he'd be. To say thank you to my grandfather.

Chapter 14

Elizabeth did come home that Saturday, just as she had promised, but I didn't get to see her. Nick and I had gone out on the horses early in the morning, and even though we were back by noon, Elizabeth had already come and gone.

She left me a note saying, "I waited and waited!" and added that she had to get back for a conference with her instructor. She also wrote that she'd be back the following Saturday. "Promise!" she wrote, and she underlined it three times, once in red ink and two times in green.

I didn't care that much really, as long as I truly knew she'd be back. But I had to admit that a part of me felt sad that she hadn't waited, that she hadn't cared to wait. Still, if she liked her school so much, that was good, because she'd want to stay.

Anyway, I knew Elizabeth and knew she couldn't help the way she acted. Probably too, it wasn't really that she didn't care, just that things happened to distract her. She was a lot like a little kid that way.

It was early morning, Sunday, when we next went out on the horses. We had ridden for hours until we came to the high hills. We were going that far because we were still looking for elk. Maura had prepared a lunch for us as she'd been doing every morning now, and even though it was only ten o'clock, we stopped to eat. I don't know why, but riding horses made me very, very hungry.

We stopped at the very top of a high hill, where the earth flattened out, kind of like a little platform — a butte, Nick called it. We hooked the horses' reins over a low branch and sat down on the ground.

I unwrapped the sandwiches, and Nick opened the Thermos and poured the hot chocolate Maura had made. I would have preferred water or something cold, but Maura said that for something cold, we could always drink out of a stream. She insisted we needed something hot to "fortify" us.

I took a slow sip of the cocoa, and then lay on my back, looking up at the sky.

Large white puffy clouds floated by in a sky so blue it looked almost fake. It reminded me of Elizabeth's paintings, her skies always super-blue, the trees stiff and straight, the sun sitting in a corner of the sky like the sun of a child's paintings. I've always thought how unreal her paintings were, but here was a sky and a sun that almost exactly matched hers. It made me wonder then why she painted pictures like that if she really hated the ranch the way she said she did.

Neither Nick nor I said much — we never did when we were out on our horses — but that day, we were even quieter than usual. I just lay and looked at the sky, and Nick lay on his stomach beside me, pulling up blades of grass.

He spoke first. "You miss your mom?" he asked.

"Kind of," I answered.

"Me, too," he said.

I turned my head to look at him.

"I mean," he said, "I miss *my* mom."

He had told me the very first day we went riding that his mom had died when he was born, so I was surprised — at first. And then I realized.

"I know," I said. "I mean, I think I know. I miss my dad, too."

"Spooky, isn't it?" Nick said.

"Missing somebody you never knew?" I said.

Nick nodded.

We were silent again for a while.

The clouds were really racing by above, blown by a wind up there that no one could see and that down on the ground, we couldn't even feel. I thought of my visits to the cemetery, how I liked to feel that my father could talk to me, that he understood the things I told him. I wondered then if my father's spirit could fly on a breeze, like a hawk. If it could, then he'd be right there with me, not just back home in the cemetery.

"Know what I think is the worst?" I said. I rolled over on my side to face him, but he was still pulling up bits of grass, so I couldn't see his face. "The worst is that you'll never know them. It's like having a twin who died when you were born or something, like a part of you is missing."

Nick nodded again. "What's it like having a mom?" he asked.

I thought about that for a minute. "I'm not sure," I said. "I mean, Elizabeth is . . . different. Not like other moms I know. What about you, what's it like having a dad?"

He looked up then and grinned at me, showing that little gap between his front teeth. "Pretty neat, I guess," he said.

I had only met his dad a few times, when we were working around the barn or when we stopped at Nick's for a drink of water or something. He was big, dark, and muscular, and he had a great smile, a lot like Nick's, with the tiny gap between his front teeth. He was always touching Nick — resting a hand on his shoulder, picking some straw out of his hair, swatting him on the behind. A nice dad, I had decided, although I had to admit that I didn't know any more about dads than Nick did about moms.

"How come your mom left before seeing you yesterday?" Nick said then.

I shrugged. "She had to get back for a conference," I said.

"You think she'll be back next week?" Nick said.

"Of course she'll be back!" I answered, and it came out really snappy sounding, much meaner than I had meant for it to sound. "She'll be back," I said more quietly.

Nick shifted, rolling over on his back to look at the sky.

There was another long, long silence between us. Suddenly I was so aware of him there next to me, of him as a person, a boy person — not like a boyfriend exactly, but definitely a friend who is a boy.

It felt so good to have a friend again.

I wondered if he felt anything like what I was feeling.

I snuck a look at him, but he was just staring at the sky and chewing on a piece of grass, as though he wasn't thinking of me at all.

For some reason, that made me sad.

What a jerk I am! Like if I decide to be friends, he has to decide the same thing at the same time.

There was another long silence, and then Nick said, "You like your grandpa?"

I nodded. "He's nice," I said.

"He likes you," Nick said.

I looked over at him. "How do you know?"

"He bought you boots."

I raised one leg and looked at my foot. My boots were scuffed and dirty already, creased into the shape of my foot, but they were so comfortable, so great for riding and for working around the barn and the paddock. Nick said I'd need rubber boots for the paddock when winter came, but I didn't like to talk about winter. Not yet. Not till Elizabeth came back, until she said for sure we were staying. Or until . . . what? Till *I* made some decision?

"When I went to thank him," I said, "know what he said?"

"What?"

" 'Go on. Out of here!' That's all he said."

"Sounds like him," Nick said, laughing.

Suddenly I heard that voice in my head, the one I had heard when I met my grandfather. "Like me," it had said. "Please like me." And I still wasn't convinced, the way Nick was, that he did like me, even if he had bought me boots.

I sighed.

"He wants you to stay," Nick said.

I sat up and hugged my knees. "He does? How do you know?"

Nick sat up, too. He reached around for his sandwich, picked it up, and took a bite, a huge bite. "I just do," he said. "I know."

He wiped his mouth with his sleeve, wiping off bits of crumbs and a shred of lettuce. He really has atrocious eating habits.

"Did he tell you that?" I insisted.

"No, he didn't tell me. I just know," he said.

"I don't think he likes kids that much."

"He likes me," Nick said.

I remembered what I had seen between him and Nick, what I had felt. "Yeah," I said. "I guess so. But that doesn't mean he likes me or wants me to stay."

Nick wiped his mouth again with his sleeve, then put his sandwich down and leaned close to me — too close. "You don't *want* him to like you?"

"I didn't say that!" I said. "I just said I don't think he does. And wipe your chin. It has mayonnaise."

Nick ran a hand over his mouth. "Would you like staying?" he asked.

I shrugged. "I don't know. If Elizabeth does."

Actually, I would love to stay, I was saying inside. I would. But what if Elizabeth decided to leave, decided she hated her art school? Then what? I sure couldn't talk to Nick — to anyone — about that problem.

Nick backed away from me, picked up his sandwich, and began eating again — messily. "You might have to stay," he said calmly.

"I don't *have* to!" I said angrily, mimicking him. "I don't have to do anything I don't feel like doing!"

"Me neither," Nick said, and suddenly he was grinning. "That's why I don't go school."

"That's different," I said. "And you should go."

It came out very prissy sounding.

But Nick was still grinning. "Why?" he said.

"So you can learn stuff," I answered.

Like table manners, I almost said, but I didn't. Even though I was mad at him, it would have been too mean, and besides, nobody teaches you table manners at school.

"I know stuff, lots of it," Nick said. "All this stuff,

145

I know." He waved his hand to show what he meant. "I know the outdoors. More than teachers know, I bet."

I didn't answer, because secretly I thought he was right. Still, it seemed like you should go to school.

"So how come it makes you mad about staying here?" Nick asked.

He was such a pain! Like a dog who wouldn't let go of a bone — or like Toby once you threw him a stick!

"It doesn't make me *mad!*" I said. I glared at him.

Right. Like I didn't sound mad!

I sighed and lay back, staring up again at the sky. "Okay," I said. "So maybe it upsets me a little."

"Why?" Nick said. "I like it here."

Yeah, I thought. And maybe that was the whole problem. Because I did, too.

Chapter 15

Weeks went by — weeks out on the horses with Nick, weeks of not seeing Elizabeth. She didn't come back those Saturdays, but she did call — every single day, she did. I missed her in some way, but I was also glad she was having fun. Because if she was liking it, maybe she would come back to the ranch to stay. And staying on the ranch was beginning to seem the most important thing to me.

One of the best parts of every day — after the riding — was evenings in the library with my grandfather. I still felt strange with him, anxious sort of. But I was beginning to like him more. And I was even able to think of him as my grandfather — not just as Sam. I couldn't say the word out loud yet, but I could in my head.

What was so wonderful about the evenings was that we talked books. I had never met anyone in the whole world, not even librarians, who loves books the way I do until I met him. Not only does he know and love books — but he knows kids' books, books I know and even books that I don't know but that he tells me about, and not just novels, either. We talked history and geography, and he's the only person I know who has ever made geography interesting. I never got the feeling that he was "teaching" me, either, as if he wanted me to catch up on my schooling, although he did mention that a few times. He said Elizabeth was really letting me down by not giving me a proper education.

Anyway, after that first week of talking books, we began to read a chapter every night to each other — or rather I mostly read to him. He can see all right to read, but by nighttime, his eyes get tired. Then he needs a magnifying glass to read and it's too hard. Besides, he says I have a pretty voice.

Me? No one had ever said that about me before, although I had been told I have a nice singing voice.

Maura always joined us in the evenings, but she sat far away from us, in a corner of the room under a special light, where she worked on her sewing, a big quilt she was making. She invited Nick to join us, but he never wanted to.

It was a Saturday, another Saturday when Elizabeth didn't come back, when we finished reading *The Yearling*. What a book! I cried my eyes out, but not in front of my grandfather. I saved it up for when I was in bed at night, and then cried like a baby.

It was my grandfather's turn to choose the book to read next and he chose *Heidi*.

Heidi! I hadn't read *Heidi* since I was about seven, and I remembered loving that book. It's a story about a girl and her grandfather, and I looked up at my grandfather when he handed me the book. Was it stupid to think what I thought then — that maybe that's why he had chosen it?

Yes. A stupid thought.

It was an old copy with a tattered cover and a beautiful cover illustration, and I smiled when I took it.

"You seem happier these days," he said.

"I do?" I said.

"You do," he answered. "Are you?"

"I guess so," I answered. I was happy — with the ranch, with Nick, with the riding. I also liked Maura a lot and even liked him, and that surprised me. I really enjoyed our times in the library. But I wasn't exactly sure about happy, I guess because I was confused: happy to be there; worried about Elizabeth.

"Do you like it here?" he continued.

"Yes, I told you that a zillion times," I said. That, at least, was true.

I opened the book.

"Hold on a minute," he said. "Let's talk."

I looked up at him.

"You never talk to me," he said.

"We talk all the time!" I answered.

"About books," he said.

I shrugged. Had he forgotten all those things I had blurted out to him about the ranch? Or did he want me to talk about Elizabeth? About staying?

"What do you want me to talk about?" I asked.

He just shrugged and kept on looking at me.

"I like it here," I said. "I told you that. I like Nick."

He smiled.

"And I like the ranch a lot," I went on.

"I can tell," he answered.

"It's so pretty out there," I said. "Do you know that the other day the sky was so blue it —"

I stopped. I had been going to say it reminded me of Elizabeth's paintings, but I didn't want to bring her up. "It was really blue," I said lamely.

"The outdoors is doing you good," he said. "You look better."

"Better?" I said. "What do you mean? Better than what?"

He pulled those dark eyebrows together. "Better than you did when you got here."

I shrugged. "I was tired then," I said. "We'd been driving for days, and besides, I was getting sick."

"You looked like something the cat dragged in," he snapped. "Elizabeth hadn't been taking proper care of you."

"You know what?" I burst out. "You say very mean things!"

"Me?" He looked genuinely surprised.

"Yes, you!"

"What are you talking about?" he asked.

"What you just said!" I tried to mimic his voice. " 'Something the cat dragged in!' Or like the time you said I was smart — but not much to look at. Or when you said my father was wild and Elizabeth is irresponsible and —"

I stopped. I had no idea I had been storing up all that stuff, no idea at all.

He was staring at me, looking as surprised as I felt at what I was saying. But surprised or no, I found myself rushing on.

"Other stuff, too!" I said. "You shouldn't say things like that my hair looks like I combed it with an eggbeater. It hurts people's feelings. How would you like it if someone told you your —"

I stopped.

"What?" he said.

I was going to say: your fingers look like bird claws.

But I just shrugged and took a deep breath. "Nothing," I said. "It's just that you shouldn't say mean things."

He means nothing by it.

As clearly as if she had just spoken, I heard the words Maura had said about him that first time we talked.

I glanced over at her.

She was looking at me as if she had sent the words across the room to me.

Embarrassed, I turned away.

I didn't mean to hurt her, to hurt her feelings. I knew she loved him. But he *shouldn't* say mean things, even if he meant nothing by it. How come he didn't know that?

There was a long silence in the room.

He put his head back against the chair, his eyes turned up to the ceiling. He began clicking his fingernails on the chair arm, just the way he had done our first day there.

It made me nervous, much more nervous than it had that first day, and I wished he'd stop it and say something. Finally he said quietly, "So you think I'm mean."

It was a statement, not a question.

"I didn't say that!" I said quietly. "I just said that you say mean things sometimes."

His eyebrows were really pulled tightly together. "Your mother used to say the same thing," he went on. "Long ago, she used to tell me I was mean."

He still had his head back against the chair, was still looking up at the ceiling. "Yes," he said, "she told me that all the time. Know what? I probably was, although God knows I didn't mean to be. It's hard to be a father — and mother — to a girl."

"You're twisting my words," I said. "I did *not* say

you were mean. I don't think you're mean. I think you're very . . . generous. Nice, even. But you do say mean things. Sometimes."

For a long minute, we looked right at each other.

"Listen," he said. "I'm an old man and —"

"No excuse!" I blurted out.

He laughed right out loud then, that super-loud laugh that always startles me.

"You're right," he said, leaning forward out of his chair and taking both my hands in his bony ones. "Being old is no excuse. But you didn't let me finish. I was going to say that I'm an old man and it takes time to change. How about we make a deal?"

"What kind of deal?" I asked.

I thought of pulling my hands away but held still.

He readjusted his position in the chair. "I'll work on holding my mean tongue," he said very seriously, although I could still see that little smile around his mouth. "And you'll do something for me."

"What?" I asked.

He was definitely smiling by then, a smile that made his face look really sweet. "Could you work on . . . getting Nick to go to school with you? It's a really good school."

Go to school, I thought. With Nick. Here!

He did want me to stay! My grandfather wanted me to stay.

Thoughts raced around inside my head. I could stay on the ranch. I could ride horses and go to school with

Nick, and at night — every single night — read stories with my grandfather and Maura. And every single night I could go upstairs to my own room, my own bed, and know that I'd never have to leave.

But what about Elizabeth?

I gently slid my hands out of his. "I'll think about it," I said.

Chapter 16

After that night, things changed between me and my grandfather. I didn't tell him I was thinking about Elizabeth, but we did talk about going to school.

For his part, he never mentioned Elizabeth either. When we were together, we both acted as if she didn't even exist.

Maura and I talked about her, though. Maura was the one who always answered the phone, so she got to talk with Elizabeth some when she called. And if I wasn't there, Maura took messages for me.

I think Maura knew I was worried because she kept reassuring me, telling me that Elizabeth would be back. She didn't think she was being obvious about it, though — I could tell. Yet I knew. She'd say things like "When your mama comes back" or "Wait till your mama sees how you learned to ride" or some such thing.

But we never talked about the future, about

Elizabeth's plans for our future. Did she want to stay? How long would she stay? Would she want to leave when she got tired of her painting school? Because I was sure of one thing: Elizabeth *would* get tired of what she was doing. I didn't know why — I never knew why — and I didn't know when. But she would, of that I was sure.

That following Saturday, the day she was again due back, I woke up early the way I always did, dressed, and went down to the kitchen. It was a windy, blustery day, the sky outside my window filled with dark, racing clouds threatening rain or snow. It didn't matter, though, because I wasn't going out riding, and I had told Nick that the day before. I was going to stay right there in case she came. I didn't want her to come and go before I got back. I didn't tell Nick that that was the reason, but I bet he knew.

Maura was already making sandwiches in the kitchen when I came down. All the dogs were gathered around her feet, and I reached under the table and patted Toby.

"How are you today, lamb?" Maura said to me.

"I'm okay," I said. I got my cereal, brought it back to the table, and sat down across from her. "I'm not going riding, though, you know," I said.

"I know," she answered, "but Nicholas will still want his lunch."

"He won't stay out long without me," I said.

Maura looked up, smiling.

I could feel myself blush. "He has really terrible table manners," I said, to cover up.

"He has no one to teach him," Maura said mildly.

"His dad could," I said.

"True, but his dad probably doesn't notice." Maura smiled. "His daddy teaches him other things, though — important things."

I nodded. I knew what she meant — Nick needed a mom.

I sighed. So did I.

I finished my cereal, and I'd just gotten up to go make some toast when Maura said, "Did you speak to your mama this morning?"

I spun around. "Speak to her? Did she call?"

"No, no, I thought you heard her. She's here — she's upstairs asleep."

"Here? She came back?"

I started for the door, started to run up and see for myself, but at the door, I stopped and turned back. She'd come down soon. She's always grouchy if I wake her up.

But she had come back! She had! I'd always known she would.

I looked over at Maura. "Is she all right?" I asked. "Everything's okay with her?"

Maura nodded, but I thought she looked troubled. "Fine, lamb, she's fine," she said. "She got in right after you went to bed last night. I thought maybe you'd heard her."

I shook my head no.

I went to the counter and made my toast, feeling myself smiling. Back — she was really, really back.

And I had so much to tell her, to show her! What would she think about our plans for school?

I came back to the table with my toast and started to sit down, but then I noticed that Maura didn't have any breakfast. "Would you like some toast?" I asked. "Want me to make some for you?"

"No, thank you, lamb," she said. "I think I'll just make myself some tea."

She started to get up, and for the first time I noticed that she had trouble getting out of the chair, just like my grandfather. She had to kind of lean on the table with one hand and use the other hand to push herself up.

It struck me then; she was old. They were both old.

"Stay there!" I said. "I'll do it."

Before she could argue, I went to the stove and put the teapot on to boil.

I got out the cup, put in the tea bag, and when the water boiled, I brought it all back to the table.

When I set the cup in front of her, Maura patted my hand gently, just the way she did sometimes with my grandfather.

"Thank you, lamb," she said quietly.

I sat down with my toast, and Maura drank her tea. We were both quiet, the only sound being the dogs scrabbling for the toast bits I was feeding them, Cody bumping her head against the table.

Elizabeth was back! And something was troubling Maura.

She was too silent, too still in the way she sat, awkward in the way she kept looking at me, and then away.

Had Elizabeth done something? Had she and my grandfather had another fight?

I was just about to ask when suddenly I heard the kitchen door swing open.

Elizabeth!

I spun around.

But it wasn't Elizabeth. It was my grandfather.

He came in looking even more fierce than usual, those eyebrows pulled tightly together.

I smiled then, remembering Maura's remark to me one day: "His bark is worse than his bite, lamb," she had said.

He came across the room to the table, pulled out a chair, and sat down across from me. Before he sat, he patted Maura's shoulder briefly, but it was almost automatic the way he did it, as if his heart wasn't really in it.

"She's back," he said abruptly, looking right at me.

"I know!" I said. "Maura told me."

"Did you talk to her?" he asked.

"No," I said. "No, I didn't."

"Well, I need to tell you something," he said.

Maura put a hand on his arm. "I think you should wait for Elizabeth," she interrupted firmly, the first time I had heard her speak like that.

It surprised me, and him, too — you could tell.

He turned to her. He looked at her for a minute, but then he shook his head slowly. "Elizabeth will have her turn," he said gently. "She always does."

"Still," Maura said. She didn't add anything more, but she kept her hand on his arm, still giving him that look, a warning kind of look.

Gently, he took her hand off his arm. "I have to do it my way," he said, and he turned back to me.

"I need to tell you something," he said again, and his voice was no longer gentle the way it had been when he spoke to Maura, although not as harsh as when he had begun. "Elizabeth is a vagabond," he said. "She has no sense of home, no sense of family. She's here, she's there, she's blown around like a leaf on a —"

"Breeze!" Elizabeth said. "Blown like a leaf on a breeze!"

She danced into the kitchen, her arms outstretched, swaying back and forth in a little dance. "Blown hither and thither!" she sang.

I jumped up.

"Sweetie!" she said.

I hurried to her.

Her arms were still outstretched in that little dance of hers, and she kept them out as I went to her. But for the first time ever, she didn't drop them when I got close to her.

"I've missed you, sweetie!" she said. And she actually hugged me.

160

"I know," I said, even though I didn't. "I've missed you, too." And that was true.

We dropped our arms, and we both stepped back.

I don't know what she was seeing, but I was seeing what I always see with her: she looked so very pretty, tiny — fragile almost, like a beautiful little doll.

Even with no makeup and her hair still rumpled from sleep, she was beautiful. And her hair was so short! She had had it cut since she left, shorter than a boy's haircut even. And still she looked like a doll.

I suddenly felt awkward.

I turned away. "Come on," I said. "Have some breakfast. Can I make you some tea?"

"Sure," she said.

I went to the stove and started her tea. But I watched over my shoulder as she went and sat at the table.

There were a lot of chairs there, but for some reason, she sat in my place, right across from my grandfather.

She pushed aside my plate, then rested her elbows on the table, her chin on her hands.

"Another glorious morning at home with my father!" she declared in this fake, gay voice.

Nobody answered. Even the dogs had stopped chewing and clamoring for food. There was complete silence in the room.

Quietly Maura got up and came over to me at the stove. "I'll do that, lamb," she said. "You go sit with your mama."

But I don't want to sit with my mama, I said to myself. Why? First I can't wait for her to get here, then, when she's here, I don't want to be near her.

I had to talk with her, though, had to find out what was going on. Slowly I started back across the room to the table.

Where to sit? Elizabeth had taken my place.

I thought of sitting next to my grandfather because that felt safe and solid. My grandfather was right — Elizabeth was here and there, blown like a leaf on the wind.

But sitting next to him, not her, would also seem like taking sides, wouldn't it?

So I didn't sit anywhere, just stood by the end of the table.

When I went over there, they both turned to me at the same moment, their heads swiveling as if they were puppets and someone had pulled a string. They started speaking at the same time, too.

"We'll pack up today," Elizabeth was saying.

"No, you won't!" my grandfather said.

"You've been out of school long enough," Elizabeth went on. "It's time we hit the road."

"Settle down, will you!" my grandfather practically roared, and he leaned so far across the table toward her that I was afraid for a moment that he'd fall right out of his chair.

I looked from one to the other.

Hit the road.

Settle down.

Meaning?

Meaning go.

162

Meaning stay.

I just shook my head, staring first at one, then at the other.

Elizabeth.

My grandfather.

I looked at Maura, and there was such a sad look on her face that I had to turn away.

My eyes swept past the window, and there I saw Nick heading for the barn. His head was down, shoulders hunched against the wind that roared out there.

Stay.

Go.

Pack up.

Settle down.

Stay.

Go.

Why had she come back? Why had I ever, ever wanted her back?

Chapter 17

It was probably wrong what I did then, but I didn't know what else to do — didn't even stop to think.

I raced to the back door, grabbed an old jacket of Maura's that was hanging there, ran outside to the barn — and almost collided with Nick.

He had just finishing saddling up Tanya and was leading her through the barn door. When he saw me, he looked surprised. "I thought you weren't going today!" he said.

I didn't answer, just shook my head.

"Hey!" he said.

It was only when he said that, when I saw his look, that I realized I was crying, that tears were streaming down my face.

"Hey! What's the matter?" he said.

I still didn't answer.

Instead, I went into Buddy's stall and began

saddling him up. I put the bridle into his mouth, tossed a blanket across his back, and threw the saddle onto him.

I wasn't being gentle with him, and he could tell. He tossed his head, blowing out his breath the way he had that first day. I knew he wasn't laughing, though. He was upset and worried.

Well, so was I.

Once I had him done up, I led him out of the barn and found Nick out there, waiting for me.

I didn't even look at him.

I just grabbed the reins, put my foot into the stirrup, and threw my leg over Buddy's back.

I clicked my tongue at him, dug in my heels, and took off.

Behind me, I could hear Tanya and Nick galloping along with us.

I've never ridden so fast, so hard. I still wasn't all that good at it, but I didn't care.

It felt terrifying. And very, very good.

The wind tore through my hair, and the trees and hills were a blur as we sped by.

I never looked back for Nick, but I could always hear him behind me, his horse matching mine.

I didn't know where I was going — just that I needed to go somewhere.

The sun was getting higher, and I could feel its warmth, yet my hands and ears were frozen. I wished so much that I had stopped for a hat and gloves.

My face was freezing, too, my cheeks wet with tears.

Every time I'd brush away the tears, they'd start all over again.

Pack up, pack up, pack up. That's what Buddy's hooves were saying: *Pack up, pack up, pack up*.

And my grandfather? He'd said no. Don't go. Settle down.

Just last week he'd said I could go to school here.

I wanted to go to school here!

But Elizabeth was leaving. I loved it here on the ranch. I liked Nick. I liked my grandfather. I liked Maura a lot.

But Elizabeth . . . She was my mother, and she had come back for me.

I clicked my tongue at Buddy and dug in my heels more, and we galloped even faster.

I don't know how far we went, me in the lead, Nick racing along behind, but it was a long, long way.

I only slowed because I was tired, because Buddy was tired. And because I didn't know what else to do.

We had come to that butte where Nick and I had picnicked that day. I slowed Buddy to a walk, then slid off his back, holding tight to his reins. He was all slathered up with sweat, and I knew I had been mean to him.

There was a stream nearby, and I led him down there to drink, Nick and Tanya following.

While the horses drank, I stood catching my breath.

I could feel Nick looking at me, but I didn't look at him.

After the horses had had their fill, we looped their

reins over a branch. I first made sure that it was a nice place, a place where there was still some grass, so Buddy could munch.

Then both Nick and I climbed the crest of the hill and sat down on a wide rock there, side by side, looking out over the valley.

For a long time, neither of us spoke — a long, long time. Every so often, I'd wipe away tears, and then they'd come again.

I kept wiping my nose and my face with my hands, and wished I had a tissue.

I dug in the pocket of Maura's jacket and found an old piece of oily rag. Disgusting. Heaven knows what Maura had used it for, but it didn't matter — it was better than nothing, and I wiped my face and eyes and nose with it.

Eventually I could feel that shaky kind of breath come over me that comes after a big cry, and I knew I was finished crying — at least for now.

I sat for another minute, till I was sure the tears were gone, and I knew what I had to do.

"I'm leaving!" I said, turning to Nick.

He didn't answer.

"How come?" he said finally.

"Because I have to."

"Why?"

"Elizabeth's going."

"So stay with your grandpa," Nick said. "He wants you. I told you that, and I'm right."

"I know," I said. "But I have to go."

I could hear him take a deep breath, almost as shaky as mine was. And then he said, "Yeah. I guess."

"You guess what?" I turned to look at him.

He shrugged. "I guess if Pa was leaving, I'd go with him, too," he said. "But it still stinks."

I nodded and I felt so relieved. It felt good to know that he understood, and I bet a lot of people wouldn't, like the teachers and kids at my school.

"Will you go to school?" I asked him suddenly, and I have no idea why I said that — unless maybe it was because I was thinking of me and my school. And what it would be like going back to Mr. Beard's class, if that's the school where I ended up.

He was quiet for a long time. "Maybe," he said finally.

"Do kids make fun of you?" I said.

"Why would they make fun of me?" he said, very mad sounding.

I shrugged. "I don't know. Except that they make fun of me."

"How come?"

"Probably the same reason they tease you," I said. "If they do tease you," I added quickly.

He didn't say anything, and I knew he was waiting for me to explain.

But how could I explain? How could anyone explain what it's like to have a family like mine — maybe even like Nick's, with a father who didn't make him go to school?

I thought of my grandfather's words: blown like a

leaf on the wind. Hither. Thither. Leave and come back, leave and go somewhere else. But that wasn't the whole reason, I knew. Maybe it's because all kids without real families — well, kids without regular families, kids like Nick and me — are all different somehow?

I leaned back, propping myself with my hands on the rock behind me, looking up at the sky.

"Maybe," I said, "maybe it's because I leave and come back, leave and come back. I used to think it was that. But now I think it's something else. But I can't explain it. I just think that whatever it is — maybe not having a regular home, not having a regular mom, someone to count on — something makes me different. I feel different." I shrugged. "Anyway, the kids think I'm strange."

"Well, you're not," he said.

"The teachers think so, too," I said.

"Well, you're not," he said again. "I think you're nice."

I kept looking at the sky but I could feel myself about to cry again. I wanted to say something nice back, but couldn't. There were lots of nice things about Nick — but I couldn't bring myself to say a single one of them. I was sure I'd burst into tears.

Nick didn't seem to be waiting. He just went on talking — and that's one of the nicest things about him. He gives a compliment as if he means it — not as if he wants one back.

"Will you come back?" he asked.

"Yes!" I said. And suddenly I knew that for sure. I'd be back. "Sometime," I said. "But I don't think Elizabeth will come."

I stood up then and looked over at the horses. Buddy was munching grass, but I could still see the sweat lathered all over him.

I started to walk over to Buddy, and Nick followed.

"Next summer?" Nick asked.

"I'll need money."

I began using the oily rag I had used as a handkerchief to wipe Buddy down. It wasn't much of a help, but it was better than nothing.

Nick stood beside me by Buddy's head, smoothing one hand up and down Buddy's neck. "You shouldn't ride a horse the way you did before, you know," he said, and he had that know-it-all tone of voice back.

Ordinarily I'd get mad, but I just shrugged. "I know," I said. "It's just that I was mad. Upset."

"You shouldn't take it out on a horse, birdbrain."

"Oh, shut up!" I said. I made my voice mad-like, but my heart wasn't really in it.

I wiped Buddy all over, murmuring to him the whole time.

Nick just stood there holding Buddy's head, rubbing behind his ears. But the way Nick kept looking over at me, I could tell he was waiting for something.

"What?" I said finally.

"When?" he asked.

"Soon. Knowing Elizabeth."

"Today?"

I shook my head. "No. Probably tomorrow."

He turned away, but before he did, I know I saw tears in his eyes.

He moved over to Tanya and began unhooking her lead, and I unhooked Buddy's. We both got on our horses.

"It's not your fault," he said then, as though he was answering something I had said — or maybe just answering a voice in his own head.

"I know," I said.

He took a deep breath, then turned away from me so that his face was hidden. "Well, so long, birdbrain," he said, so quietly that I could hardly hear him.

And then he whirled Tanya around and took off.

"Hey!" I said. "Wait up!"

But he was gone. And the way he was riding, I knew I'd never catch up.

I watched him go, feeling my tears start up all over again.

"So long, birdbrain!" I whispered after him. I raised a hand and waved, even though he was already almost out of sight. "So long!"

Chapter 18

If it had been up to Elizabeth, she would have left that very afternoon, but she agreed on the next day when I insisted that I had too many things to do. I didn't really, but I made up things — that I had to work in the barn, clean up my saddle and stuff — things I could do in twenty minutes, but Elizabeth didn't have to know that.

But I needed the time because I had to say good-bye, not only to Maura and Nick and my grand-father — but to things. To Buddy. The barn. The ash tree. The ravine.

There was a heaviness in my chest, the same kind of feeling I sometimes get in my throat, as if I need to cry but can't.

I spent the whole rest of that day out riding — gently. I was very slow with Buddy. And I rode alone. Partly that was because I wanted to, and partly because

I didn't see Nick anywhere. I was pretty sure he was avoiding me, but that was okay. I understood.

When late afternoon came, I went back to the house to pack up. I got Toby's box from the cellar, where it had been stored, and searched the house till I found his favorite stuffed dog. I put those things together by the back door, then went up to my room to pack my things.

Maura had done all my laundry, and it was all clean and folded and stacked on my bed. In the pile with my things were all the sweaters and sweatshirts she had been lending me all these weeks for riding.

I separated out her things and set them aside, then packed my own. The only one of hers I kept was the first one, the University of Colorado one she had lent to me, gave to me, she'd said, that first day after I'd been sick. I would wear that one when we left.

While I was packing, Elizabeth was packing, too, and I could hear her in the next room, whistling and humming. I'd meet her on the stairs or in the hall, and she was always smiling and bopping around, the way she always did when we were getting ready for a trip.

"Don't look so grim!" she said to me once as we passed on the stairs.

I didn't answer.

I wasn't grim. Just sad.

When I was just about all packed, Maura came to my room. She stood in the door for a moment, watching me. "Those other shirts are yours, too, lamb," she said, nodding at the pile of things I had set aside.

"They're yours," I said.

"I want you to have them," she said.

I nodded. "Thanks," I said. And I put them with my things in the bag. I would like to have them, not just because they were warm and nice, but because they reminded me of her.

"Your grandfather would like you to come to the library, lamb," she said quietly. "Would you be good and run down and see him for a moment?"

I nodded. "Okay," I said. "Is he still mad?"

She shook her head. "Not at you." She looked around, then came further into the room, and closed the door gently behind her. "Not at you," she repeated. "Perhaps at your mama."

"They're always mad at each other, aren't they?" I said.

She nodded.

"How come?" I asked.

She sat down heavily on the bed next to my backpack, gently running one hand over my pile of things that were still waiting to be packed. "Old hurts," she said. "Some people nourish old hurts. I think he's mad at her for leaving long ago, and for not staying in touch. And her . . ."

Maura looked out the window, a faraway look in her eyes, as if maybe she was seeing something far away too. "I don't know Elizabeth real well," she said. "But I have a feeling she's mad at him because he wasn't enough for her when she was young — maybe not enough of a parent. Maybe like he said, she wanted him to be father and mother, too. And he couldn't."

I looked out the window too, thinking. Did I do that, too? Was I disappointed in Elizabeth because I wanted her to be a mother and a father, too? I didn't think so. I thought I just wanted her to be a mother.

And I didn't think she did that real well, either. I sighed.

"They just go over and over those hurts," Maura said, still looking out the window. "Now you" — she turned to me — "you're different. You forgive. You go on."

Did I — do I — forgive? Go on?

"How do you know that?" I said.

"Because you're going with your mom," she said.

But I wasn't sure she was right that that meant I'd forgiven her.

Maura reached in the pocket of her apron then and took something out. "Now, lamb," she said quietly. "I want you to have something. Do you have a safe place, a private place for something?"

"In my backpack." I nodded at it lying there beside her.

"Your mama won't look there?"

"I don't think so. She never has."

"Then take this and put it away, all right?"

She handed me a small green change purse, leather with a gold clasp. It was soft, and I knew right away it was good leather, not cheap plastic.

"Open it," she said.

I did. Inside was money. Lots of it. More money than I had seen in one place in my whole entire life. There wasn't just change in there, either, but bills, and they weren't one dollar bills. They were tens and twenties.

Why? I looked up her.

"You might need it," she said. "There's two hundred dollars there, tens and twenties. And in here" — she took the purse from me and showed me a small section — "in here, another hundred, a hundred dollar bill. Save that. That's for emergencies only. And here's our address and phone number and telephone credit card number. You come back here anytime you need or want. You understand?"

For a long moment, I held the card, looking at the phone number and the credit card number. She had written out directions for using it, too: push "O" for Operator. Wait for tone. Punch in the number. Wait for tone. Punch in the number again, followed by four numbers. And then I would get her. She would answer and say, "Is that you, lamb?"

And I would say, "Yes, it is me. Lamb."

I could feel tears forming in my eyes.

I stuffed the purse deep in the bottom of my backpack, then swallowed hard and turned away. "I'll go to the library now," I said.

Maura got up from the bed and followed me out of the room, and I ran down the stairs.

When I opened the library door, I was surprised to

see that my grandfather wasn't in his usual place by the fireplace. He was standing by the window looking out, his back to the room.

He must have known I was there, though, because as soon as I came in, he began to speak — although he didn't turn around.

"You could go to school here," he said softly, and all the usual gruffness was gone from his voice. "Nick could go with you. It's really quite a fine school. And you can ride anytime you want. Buddy can be your very own horse. Of course, anytime she wants, Elizabeth could come visit you, stay even. I know she's not real fond of this place, or of me, but maybe she'd learn to tolerate us. If you were here."

I didn't answer.

He waited for a moment, and then went on. "And when winter comes," he said, "the ranch is even more beautiful, with the snow and ice. When the sun shines on the snowfields, you have to close your eyes it sparkles so much. I'd have to get you special sunglasses, eye protection, for when you go riding. And then there are the nights when it snows, and you hear the storm outside. We get drifts that pile as high as the roof in places. And when you ride the horses, the snow is up to their flanks. It's an incredible sight — it almost looks like they're swimming."

He paused again, but still didn't turn from the window.

Grandfather, I can't stay, I wanted to say. *Grandfather . . .*

But in all the time we'd been here, the weeks and now months — I still couldn't call him that out loud, could only think it.

Since he wouldn't turn to me, I went up beside him then, stood right there next to him, looking out the window — looking at the hills turning blue in the twilight, the setting sun flinging streaks of purple and red across the sky.

"Before I came here," I said, "I used to dream about this ranch. I even . . . this is embarrassing . . . but I even dreamed about you! I used to dream that you sent for me to come live with you, that this place was my home."

I stopped.

"But you're leaving," he said.

"She needs me," I answered.

"What do you need?"

He turned to face me then, and we just looked at each other for a long time.

I realized then how different he was from my mind picture of him before we'd come — so tall, so thin, so fierce looking, and old too, older than I had thought. But better-looking than the Marlboro Man. I had gotten to like the way he looked, even liked the way he frowned down at me.

So what did I need?

I thought for a minute, twisting my baby ring, my good-luck ring, round and round my little finger. What did I need? A home. Love, everybody needs love. A family. Somebody to want me.

"She's my mother," I said. "She's my mother and she's weird sometimes and she makes me mad just like she makes you mad. But she's mine. She's my home, too."

He frowned even deeper than before. "Believe it or not, I admire your mother," he said.

I just stared at him.

"She had you, she raised you, she stuck by you in her own way. And look how you turned out."

He moved away from me then, leaning heavily on his cane.

At first, I thought he was just walking out on me, he moved so abruptly. But he just went to the table, and came back with a book — *Heidi*.

"I won't be able to say good-bye in the morning," he went on, and that gruff voice was back again. "But take this. Keep it." He held the book out to me. "Keep it till you come back. Will you come back?"

"Yes. But what if Elizabeth won't?"

"I'll send you plane tickets," he said.

"You will? For when?"

"For whenever you want them. Christmas. Summer. Whenever you want."

I took a deep breath.

I could come back! Anytime I wanted.

He was holding the book out, and I took it from his hands, but then I had a thought, the same terrible thought Heidi had when she had to leave for that long, awful winter: what if the old grandmother died before she could return?

I looked up at him and blurted it out, feeling like a fool. "You won't die, will you?" I said. "You won't die before I come back?"

He laughed suddenly, that same deep laugh that had surprised me so that first day. "I'm not planning on dying yet!" he said gruffly.

He bent close to me then, laying one finger gently on my cheek. "No one knows how long any of us will live," he said. "But as long as I have breath, I'm here for you. The ranch is here, and Maura's here. And I'm here. You can count on that. You can count on me."

Yes. Yes. I believed that.

I could count on him.

Chapter 19

It was super-early when Elizabeth woke me next morning, so early it was even darker than the mornings when I got up with Nick. But Elizabeth was already dressed and ready to go, running in and out with things for the car. It was so early that even the dogs were still in their beds by the stove when I went into the kitchen, although they kept eyeing me, as if they thought it might be time for food.

Maura was making sandwiches, just as though it was any other morning. "For you and your mama," she said when she saw me. "Something for the road."

I nodded. I went to the cabinet for my cereal, then brought it to the table and sat down across from her, just the way I had for so many mornings now.

Through the window, I could see Elizabeth moving around outside. She had pulled the car right up to the house and was fussing around with the trunk, loading up all her paintings. I hadn't asked what happened at the painting school, because it didn't matter. Probably she had gotten tired of it, was all.

I took a few bites of my cereal, then pushed the plate away and stood up. I really wasn't very hungry.

"It's all right," Maura said as if I had spoken out loud. She got up, too. "There's lots of food for later, sandwiches and apples and cookies. I even packed some treats for Toby."

I tried to smile at her, but I could feel my lip tremble.

Cody and Monte suddenly started barking, and Toby even joined in. All three of them scrambled from their beds and stood by the back door, growling low in their throats, as if they were protecting us against marauders outside. But it was only Elizabeth.

"You ready?" she said to me, looking around. "You got Toby?"

"I'll be ready in a minute," I said, because I wanted to say good-bye to Maura, and I didn't want to do it in front of her.

Elizabeth nodded. "I'll wait for you in the car," she said. She turned to Maura, and Maura held out the lunch to her. "Thanks, Maura," Elizabeth said. "Thanks for everything." And then she went outside carrying the lunch and Toby's box.

I looked at Maura and she looked back. Then she put both arms out to me and I walked right into her arms and she closed them around me. Funny, how good it felt. She was soft to hug, and she held me close and said softly, "There, there, lamb — there, there," as if she thought I was crying, but I wasn't, although I was awfully close to it.

Then she held me away from her and looked right into my eyes. "Go on, now," she said, pushing me gently toward the door. "It won't get any easier. Just do it. You'll be back. Don't grieve."

Then she bent and scooped Toby up and handed him to me. "God bless," she said, and she practically pushed me out of the door.

In the car, I put Toby gently into his box in the backseat, and Elizabeth started up the car.

Once again, Elizabeth and I were on our way.

We began bumping down the drive then, making the long, sweeping turn past the out-buildings, past the barn where the horses would still be sleeping, past the little gray house where Nick lived with his dad.

I looked around, feeling that lump in my throat, that choking sensation I had had since yesterday. I was saying good-bye to so much — not just people, but the fields and ravines, the horses and deer, the ash tree and the sky. I would miss the mountains — I knew their names now — I'd miss the sky, the coyotes, the jackrabbits, the . . . everything.

I turned and watched over my shoulder as we drove down that drive. All the way down, I watched my grandfather's house recede into the distance, till all I could see was the tiny patch of light in the kitchen. I pictured Maura at the stove making tea, fondling Monte and Cody, pictured my grandfather appearing in the doorway, that deep frown between his eyes. I pictured them there — there for me.

You can count on me, he had said.

I am counting on you, I said silently to them. I added something else then, something important. *I'm coming back,* I said silently. *You can count on me.*

And then I turned around to face front — to face whatever it was Elizabeth and I would do next. Together.

About the Author

PATRICIA HERMES has written twelve books for young people. Her novel *You Shouldn't Have to Say Good-bye* was the recipient of the California Young Reader Medal, the Iowa Young Reader Medal, the Michigan Pine Tree Book Award, and the Hawaii Nene Award. In the same tradition, *Mama, Let's Dance* received rave reviews and was named a *School Library Journal* Best Book of the Year.

Ms. Hermes is the mother of five grown children and lives in Fairfield, Connecticut.